Still A Dog

Still A Dog

Mark Anthony

www.urbanbooks.net

Urban Books, LLC
78 East Industry Court
Deer Park, NY 11729

ISBN 13: 978-1-60162-509-0
ISBN 10: 1-60162-509-X

First Mass Paperback Printing June 2012
First Trade Paperback Printing September 2009
Printed in the United States of America

10 9 8 7 6 5 4 3 2

Distributed by Kensington Publishing Corp.
Submit Wholesale Orders to:
Kensington Publishing Corp.
C/O Penguin Group (USA) Inc.
Attention: Order Processing
405 Murray Hill Parkway
East Rutherford, NJ 07073-2316
Phone: 1-800-526-0275
Fax: 1-800-227-9604

Over ten years ago, I sat down at a computer and I wrote *Dogism*. I wrote *Dogism* with no intentions of ever publishing it. But as fate would have it, *Dogism* was published and since that time I've written and published more books than I ever could have imagined. One rule that I had set for myself was that I would never write a sequel to any book that I had written. But I was inspired to write the sequel to *Dogism*, in part because there was a particular message that I wanted to get across in this book using the gift of writing that I have been blessed with. I also wanted to write this book as a reward to myself for years of hard work, perseverance and faith, which is truly the only way to any kind of success in life. So I dedicate this book to myself as well as to all of the readers who have supported me over the years and to those people who diligently, with self-discipline, work very hard at whatever it is that they truly love to do.

Prologue

It had been six years since I had confessed the life-changing news to my wife Nicole. It was devastating and deal-breaking news, news that would have ended most marriages in a heartbeat. The news was that I, Lance Thomas, at the time a husband of five years, had gotten another woman pregnant! Surprisingly—and shockingly—my wife had actually forgiven my black ass.

Nicole was a good Christian wife in every sense of the word. And after she had forgiven me for such a horrendous act of disloyalty, I did everything within my power to recommit myself to her and to God.

Unfortunately, the thing that I didn't realize was that infidelity never truly dies. The DNA of infidelity is sort of like the leaves on a tree. For a season the leaves on a tree dry up and fall to the ground, but the tree itself isn't dead, which means that in the upcoming spring season new leaves will take the place of all of the old leaves that fell to the ground.

In my case, the leaves of infidelity had fallen out of my life. They fell to the ground and the season of being faithful and true to myself, and to my marriage, lasted for all of six years. Despite some drama here and there, those six years were very good years and I didn't necessarily want them to end. But in life, all good things must come to an end and with me, after six years of doing the right thing, that season had come to an end and I had entered into a new season of Dogism.

This new season of Dogism would be different, though. Fortunately for me I had learned some things from my past. Sort of like rules that I would use to help me govern the seeds of infidelity that had sprung back to life.

Rule 1: Don't be Sloppy!

I knew that venturing down that familiar path would mean that I would diligently have to cover my tracks and not make any mistakes. In fact, I couldn't afford to make even one mistake or else my marriage would definitely end.

Rule 2: Never Snitch on Yourself!

John Gotti once said that if he were to rob a church and if the pope and the police were to catch him red-handed coming out of the church with the loot in his hand, and a steeple, and a cross sticking out of his ass that he would still never admit to robbing the church!

That John Gotti comment was always funny as hell to me but I came to understand the twisted wisdom in what he was saying about not snitching on yourself. It took some time for me to understand why snitching on myself was so stupid, but like any mistake, mistakes are designed to teach us something and we can eventually use that mistake to our benefit. During those six years that followed the revelation of my infidelity, there were many nights I spent consoling my wife and trying to do whatever I had to do in order to restore trust in our marriage. And I would be lying if I said that I didn't repeatedly want to kick myself for having opened my mouth and told on myself. Yeah, I knew that because I told on myself and hadn't actually been caught cheating that it was a plus in proving my sincerity to do right. But at the same time, I came to realize that keeping what's done in the dark-in the dark, actually helps avoid a whole lot of pain and misery!

Rule 3: Don't Break Rules One and Two!

Chapter One

They say that fate is when preparation meets opportunity. Well, as fate would have it, I just happened to be in the city of Philadelphia promoting a new book that I had written for The Unit when I walked into the DNC bank that was located on the corner of Broad and Locust in downtown Philly, and I was presented with the opportunity of a lifetime.

I was planning on just running into the bank to use the ATM but I looked to my left and I saw the most gorgeous bank teller that I had ever seen in my life. She was the spitting image of the singer Ciara, only she appeared to be a bit thicker. Her eyes were the first thing that had caught my eye when she looked up and glanced toward my direction. From a distance I could tell that she had either hazel or green eyes because they were just piercing right through me but in a very soft, non-menacing, non-seductive way, but still piercing.

Just as quickly as she had looked in my direction, her eyes then shifted away from me. She took her right hand and moved some of her long black hair away from her forehead and shifted it behind her right ear. Since it was slow in the bank, she lifted a book that she had in front of her and started to read it.

Her presence and the whole scene reminded me so much of when I first met my ex-mistress Toni, six years ago while driving down a Brooklyn street one sunny afternoon.

"Lance, just keep it moving, nigga," I said to myself as I contemplated whether or not I should say something to the beautiful teller and make the most of this once-in-a-lifetime opportunity.

I had just taken out four hundred dollars from the ATM, so I had gotten what I'd came for, but yet it was incredibly hard for me to just turn around and walk the hell out of the bank. It was like the teller was calling my name or something.

Lance, keep it moving! I said more forcefully to myself.

I counted my money to make sure that it was all there. After putting the money into the pocket of my Artful Dodger jeans I walked out of the bank. Every ounce of me began to burn with regret and with curiosity. I walked about half a block, and when I got to the corner, I waited for the green light to turn red so that I could cross the street.

The light turned red and the crowd of pedestrians crossed the street and went on about their business. But I stood still in my tracks on a freezing cold and blustery afternoon trying to decide if I should go back into the bank and talk to the girl that I had just seen.

"A'ight, so what I'll do is just go in and introduce myself to her but I won't ask for the number," I said to myself, still trying to convince myself to do something that I knew I should just leave the hell alone.

Giving in to my weakness, I blew air out of my lungs, turned back around and headed back to DNC bank. The bank was surprisingly empty, considering that it was lunchtime and there were a bunch of office workers and businesses in that area. But that was cool, because it gave me more of an opportunity to figure out just how I was gonna make my move.

The teller that I wanted to talk to had a customer at her window so I chilled for a minute near the customer service desk, where I calmly slid off my wedding ring and slipped it into my pocket before going in for the kill. I had no idea what I was going to say to her, but I was determined to be as smooth as possible.

After about two minutes or so she was finished helping the customer that was at her window and I wasted no time and I moved right in.

"Hello, how are you doing today?" she asked with a smile that could have lit up any dark room. She had perfect white teeth.

"Oh, I'm good. I'm cold as hell, but other than that I'm good."

"Yeah, it is freezing outside. This weather is crazy. I hate the wintertime," she added, trying to be as polite and friendly as possible.

I looked at the name tag that she had clipped to her blouse to see what her name was and she smiled and playfully pointed to her head and said, "umm . . . up here, I'm here."

"Oh, nah, I wasn't looking at your chest, I was just looking at your name tag."

She laughed and said, "I'm just messing with you, so how can I help you?"

I reached into my pocket and pulled out five twenty-dollar bills and asked her if I could have one hundred dollars in singles.

"Sure. No problem."

"So I see you're reading *My Woman His Wife*," I said to her while she counted the money.

She nodded her head to acknowledge my comment but she didn't speak, looking as if she was trying not to lose her count. But as soon as she finished counting the money, she did reply.

"This book is so good it's gonna get me fired. It's so good! I love Anna J. That's my girl!"

"Yeah, it's a good book. The sex scenes are crazy."

"Well, I'm hooked on it and so are all of my coworkers."

"You know, I'm actually a writer too."

The teller looked at me with twisted lips and a smirk on her face, "What books have you wrote? You're not a writer."

"No, I swear to God, I am. I wrote three books. Actually, that's why I'm in Philly. I'm from New York but we got a book signing tonight and then a book release party for my new joint I did with The Unit Books."

"The Unit? They doing books now too?"

"Yup."

"Really, so what's your name?"

"Lance Thomas, I wrote—"

"Stop lying! *Lady's Night,* right?" she asked while cutting me off.

"Yeah," I replied with a smile.

"I so don't believe you. Oh my God! That's one of my favorite books ever. Matter fact, let me see some ID."

I started to laugh and I said again that it was really me.

"Okay, so if it is then let me see your ID."

I reached into my wallet and I took out my driver's license and showed it to her.

"Oh, my God! I can't believe this," she said while smiling from ear to ear.

"Mashonda Williams, that's you, right?" I asked. The chemistry between me and Mashonda was off the meter—at least to me it was—but I was sure that she was feeling me just as much as I was feeling her.

She nodded her head, yes.

"See, I really was looking at your name tag." I joked and said, "So, Mashonda, what are you doing later? Why don't you come to the book signing for my new book; it's gonna be at the Borders in the Gallery at seven o'clock."

"Tonight? At the Gallery? That's so funny, because I heard them talking about that on the morning show on the radio."

"Yeah, it's tonight. And I already know that you're a reader, so if you don't come I'm really gonna be offended."

Mashonda laughed and she assured me that she would definitely come through with one of her homegirls.

I took one of her business cards that was on the counter and I took hold of the pen that was also on the counter. I wrote my name and cell phone number on the back of her card and gave it to her.

"I know where you work so if you don't show up I'm gonna be back here tomorrow to stalk you and harass you. Here's my number. Call me anytime. Okay?"

Mashonda smiled and she nodded her head. And then there was this awkward silence.

I broke the silence by saying, "My money. You never gave it to me."

"Oh! I'm so sorry. I'm really trippin,' " she said while handing me the money. "And don't be giving those strippers all your money either," she joked.

"Guilty as charged," I said, smiling.

Before turning to leave, I made a phone with my thumb and my index finger and silently mouthed the words *call me*.

Mashonda nodded her head and I continued walking out of the bank. And just like that I knew that I had Mashonda exactly where I wanted her.

Chapter Two

When I made it back to my hotel I went up to my room and laid down on the bed and flipped through the cable channels with the remote. It was barely three o'clock and I was bored as hell, trying to kill some time before heading over to the book signing later that evening. I decided to order some food and some Heineken's from room service. As soon as I was done ordering, my wife called me.

"Hey, Nicole."

"Hey, baby, I'm just checking up on you, letting you know that I miss you."

I laughed into the phone. "You miss me already? I only been gone for one night. I guess I must be putting in down right, huh?"

"Shut up. You so stupid. So what are you up to?"

"Nothing, I'm just bored as hell. I ain't even really hungry but I ordered room service to try and kill some time."

"So you just eating to eat?"

"It's all good. The publishing company is covering the tab, so why shouldn't I eat?"

"You are too much."

"So what's up with you? You had to go to court today?"

"No, I'm just in the office working on this motion and it's killing me. I wanna get outta here by five but I know I probably won't leave here until seven. I just want to get this outta my hair. So listen, what are you doing later, after the signing?"

"Well, I'm gonna go to the release party and then I'm bouncing."

"Oh, okay, so you'll be home tonight at what, probably around four or five in the morning?"

"Yeah, something like that."

"Okay, so be safe. And remember, LL has his game in the morning."

"Oh, I forgot about that. At eleven, right? Yeah, okay, I'll definitely be back by then."

"Okay, so I'll let you go. You being good, right?"

"Yeah, Nicole, of course."

"I'm just checking, you know that's part of my job. Okay, so be good. Call me when you heading out no matter how late it is. I love you."

"I love you too."

With that, I hung up, and I knew that Nicole's only reason for calling me was to ask me if I was being good and to remind me to be good. And for the most part I can't say that I blame her. I mean, after all, I had cheated on her back in the days when I was just a lowly blue-collar worker, so now that I was a bestselling author, travelling from state to state and going to party after party without her, I was sure that there were constantly thoughts in the back of her head that made her wonder if I could be faithful through all of the potential temptation.

And to my credit, so far I had been faithful. I can't say that it was easy but I was holding up. My ex-mistress Toni had moved on and she was now married to a successful record producer, so that helped me stay on the right track. My other mistress, the stripper Scarlett, moved miles away to Atlanta, had two kids by two different dudes, and she got fat as a house, so by default she removed herself from my lust radar.

But as far as I was concerned, Toni and Scarlett were old news to me. It was like a been-there, conquered-that type of thing. Everyday I was tempted to conquer something new, but so far I had held that temptation in check. Unfortunately, I knew that when it came to Mashonda, she represented something fresh, something new and something exciting. I had to conquer her just to satisfy that urge that was in me.

Mashonda was gonna be a problem for me. I knew she was, but like a dumb-ass I was willing to take whatever chance I needed to take in order to satisfy that urge that I had in me to get with her.

Chapter Three

By the time seven o'clock rolled around, I had been escorted from my hotel to Borders bookstore in the Gallery Mall for the launch of The Unit Books. I was accompanied by the fellow The Unit writers: Angie Santiago and Lameek and the superstar rappers Fifth Ward and Purple Hayes.

All day long, all of the Philly hip-hop stations had been promoting the event at the Gallery, but never in my wildest dreams did I expect to see the mob of people that were in the mall trying to get inside the bookstore. Of course, I knew that Fifth Ward's name was what had brought out all the throngs of people, but it didn't matter because by default I would be receiving a lot of the attention as well.

Security managed to get us safely into the bookstore and the managers of the bookstore took us to our table and instructed us on how things were going to proceed. And as soon as we sat down and began to autograph books for the massive line of customers, my cell phone began vibrating. I looked down and I saw that I had a text from Mashonda.

Hi Lance, this is Mashonda, the girl you met in the bank today. If you can, please call me back at this number 267-999-5454?

Although I was preoccupied signing books, I wasted no time and called her right back.

"Hello?"

"Hi, Lance. Listen, you didn't tell me that all of these people were gonna be here. Security is telling me that unless I had already purchased a book from earlier in the day that I can't get in. They saying I need some kind of bracelet or a tag or something in order to get in."

"Where are you?"

"I'm outside the mall at the main entrance."

"Okay, listen, I'm gonna get you in, don't worry. This line is really crazy so I'm gonna pass the phone to one of the security guards and have him come get you. Just don't hang up. Give me a minute, though. A'ight?"

"Okay, no problem."

I quickly got up and got the attention of one of the plainclothes security guards that had escorted us into the bookstore. I explained to him the situation and told him that I really needed him to do me the favor of going to the main entrance and getting Mashonda. He was cool about it and gave me no problem. He took hold of the phone and began talking to her to find out exactly where she was and what she was wearing.

Fifteen minutes later the security guard came back to the store, along with Mashonda and one of her friends.

I know that I looked like a superstar because there was a horde of photographers and video cameramen who were all positioned behind a roped-off section of the bookstore and as we signed books the photographers continually snapped pictures so there were nonstop camera flashes. The crowd mixed with the chicks who were screaming, crying, and taking off their panties for Fifth Ward while they got their books signed.

Mashonda smiled and she waved a little nervous smile to me as I motioned for her to skip the line and to come to where I was at. She walked toward me with her friend. I stood up and walked around to the other side of the table and she gave me a quick hug.

"Heyyy, so I guess you really are a writer," she joked.

Mashonda had on a chinchilla jacket that came to her waist. She had on a skintight pair of black Citizen jeans and some high-heel boots that came up to her knees. Her ass, thighs, and hips were off the hook. Being that she had been behind the counter at the bank, I had never gotten a chance to see her full body so I was seeing it for the first time, and I was loving what I was seeing.

"Lance, this is Connie. She works with me at the bank; she reads everything just like me."

"Nice to meet you," I said as I extended my hand to Connie's and shook it.

"Well, here, let me get y'all a copy of the books. Do y'all want them signed?"

Mashonda and Connie both nodded their heads and followed me back to the table where I signed my book for them and then passed it to Fifth, Angie Santiago, and Lameek for them to sign as well.

"Fifth, this is Mashonda and Connie," I said as I introduced the two gorgeous women to Fifth.

"Nice to meet y'all," Fifth replied as he signed their books.

Connie was beaming from ear to ear and she whispered something into Mashonda's ear.

"Lance, do you mind if we get a picture with you?" Mashonda asked.

I posed for the picture with the two of them and then I asked Fifth if he would get in the picture as well. They handed the security guard their camera phones and asked him if he would take the pictures for them. After we had taken the pictures, my publicist was looking at me with this look to kill; she wanted me to focus and get back to business.

"Listen, Mashonda," I said, discreetly talking low and directly into her ear, "when we leave here we're heading over to Ms. Tootsie's to eat and then we're gonna go to Pinnacle's for the release party. I know I don't really know you from Adam, but I want you to hang out with me tonight. I gotchu on everything; drinks, food, whatever you want, I gotchu."

Without hesitation, Mashonda nodded her head and said, "Yeah, no doubt. That's what's up." Then she spoke to Connie and relayed to her what I had said and the two of them both agreed to roll with us after we left the bookstore.

Mashonda and Connie roamed throughout the mall and window-shopped until the book-signing event was over. At eight-thirty I called her on her cell phone and told them to meet us in the rear entrance of the mall that lead into the parking lot. They linked up with us and we all piled into a white, stretch Hummer that the publishing company had booked for us and we made our way over to Ms. Tootsie's.

Ms. Tootsie's was rammed beyond capacity but they knew that we were coming through so they had tables reserved for us. We ate like kings and queens as every eye in the place was on us. Throughout the whole time I had to give it to Mashonda and Connie, because they both knew how to act and weren't acting all brand-knew and starstruck like they had never been anywhere before. At the same time, they talked, made jokes, and came across like they were real comfortable.

"Y'all drink?" I asked Mashonda and Connie over the loud music in the club.

"Like a fucking fish!" Connie laughed and said.

"No, *you* drink like a fish; I ain't no alcoholic like that," Mashonda corrected her friend.

Just by the way Mashonda was dressed I could tell that she was used to hanging with ballers. I highly doubted that she got that five thousand-dollar outfit from her ten dollar an hour bank salary, so my guess was she was used to niggas tricking on her. She definitely had the look to accommodate it.

As usual, the food at Ms. Tootsie's was off the chain, but we couldn't stay there as long as we wanted to because we had to make it over to Pinnacle's for the party. By the time we got to the club, it was past eleven-thirty and the spot was rammed. All of the attention was on our entourage as the bouncers held the ropes open so that we could enter. The attention stayed on us as we made our way to the VIP section.

We walked over to the leather couches and Mashonda sat down very ladylike. But Connie, on the other hand, wasted no time in standing on the headrest of the couch and started dancing to the music.

"I guess you can see that she's the wild one out of the bunch!" Mashonda shouted into my ear.

"Nah, it's cool, I like her style," I replied as I attempted, and got ahold of one of the waitresses and ordered a bottle of Patrón and apple martinis for Connie and Mashonda. Almost on cue, as soon as I sat down next to Mashonda, I felt my cell phone vibrating. I looked at it and it was Nicole calling me. I would've picked up but there was just way too much noise in the club so I let it go to voice mail. And besides the noise, I didn't answer my phone because I just didn't want to speak to Nicole. See, I knew what I was plotting on doing and whenever I was doing wrong I would try and completely block out thoughts of my wife so that I wouldn't feel guilty.

"Yo, so can I be straight up with you and tell you that I was stalking you at the bank today?" I said into Mashonda's ear.

"Stop lying," she said and laughed.

"I swear to God I was! But I know you probably get customers all day long trying to talk to you. Especially with that tight-ass toddler shirt you had on," I joked.

"Yeah, it gets so annoying and draining at times."

"Why is that? Oh, let me guess, 'cause you got a man and you all loyal and in love with him, right?"

Mashonda just smiled. But she didn't respond to my statement about her having a man. I continued with the small talk with her for about another fifteen minutes, and that was all the time that it took for the Patrón to start flowing through my system and for me to really step my game up.

The DJ was playing a bunch of old school hits so the vibe was crazy.

"So, listen, when I leave I'm heading to the Four Seasons. I got a room there and then I'm bouncing in the morning, going back to New York, but I don't wanna leave you. I still wanna chill witchu some more tonight."

Mashonda sipped on her drink and she looked at me and nodded her head. She then sat her drink down, stood up, grabbed me by the hand and pulled me up so that I could dance with her.

"You know I don't know you like that to be going back to your room with you," she said into my ear as I did a two-step to the music while she danced much harder than I was dancing.

Just the breath from her mouth grazing my earlobe had my dick standing at attention.

"I know it's not just me, but don't you feel like we knew each other for a minute? Like it's a connection or something, right or wrong?" I smiled and said, "The chemistry is crazy, just admit that shit."

Mashonda smiled and then screamed into my ear while slurring her words, "Yeah, I gotta admit that it iszzzkinda crazy."

I could tell the two drinks that Mashonda had were getting to her, besides the fact that she was talking extremely too loud and slurring her words. She just had this seductive look in her eyes and it was a completely different look than I had seen when I saw her at the bank earlier.

She placed her hand behind my neck and pulled me closer to her. "You smell real good."

I didn't say anything, but I was hoping like hell that her friend Connie wasn't the cock-blocking type, because Mashonda was turning me on like a motherfucka, and I was gonna do whatever I had to do to get her to come back to my room with me.

"It does feel like I've met you before, or something. You're right about that," Mashonda said, laughing. Two seconds after the DJ switched up the music and threw on a reggae song I pulled her body up against my body, and she started grinding on me. My dick was hard as hell and I know she felt that shit.

"So you good, right?"

"Nah, I'm scared of your ass," she replied.

"Why?"

She looked at me and nodded her head, and she continued to grind on me. She started to massage my dick through my pants.

"That's why," she replied.

"You play dirty, but I like that."

She didn't respond; she just turned her back to me and dipped her body low and then came back up and started backing her ass up on my dick. She was fucking driving me crazy.

Right at that moment my BlackBerry began buzzing again. I looked at it and it was Nicole texting me, telling me not to forget to call her when I left.

"You drove with Connie or y'all drove separate?"

"I drove, we came together," Mashonda said as she turned back around and faced me and continued grinding on me.

I scanned the crowded VIP area until I got Lameek's attention and motioned for him to come over to where I was at.

"What's the deal, my nigga?"

"Yo, I'm trying to bounce with shorty and take her back to the spot, but her homegirl Connie that was at the restaurant with us, I'm not trying to leave with her. So I need you to take this sixty dollars and make sure she gets home. But just chill with her for me and make sure she has a good time, you feel me?"

"No doubt, I gotchu my dude," Lameek said and gave me a pound.

I took Mashonda by the hand and quickly made my rounds through the VIP area and told Fifth, Hayes, and my agent that I was bouncing but that I would get up with them. They all saw me holding Mashonda's hand so they all knew what was up without me having to explain anything.

Mashonda wanted another drink on our way out. We stopped at the bar at the front of the club, and she ordered vodka and cranberry juice and I ordered a Hennessy on the rocks.

"You shouldn't be mixing drinks like that, that's how you throw up," I warned.

"I'm grown, don't worry," Mashonda said as she winked at me.

After we finished our drinks, we made it out to the car. I gave the driver forty dollars and told him that I was bouncing early but everybody else was staying until later. So without hesitation he opened the door for us and took us to my hotel room.

As soon as we walked into my room, I was thinking about turning on the TV and doing the whole small talk thing, but I could sense that shit was just different. The vibe and the chemistry was bananas so I knew that I was gonna go right for the kill.

"Let me take your coat," I said to her as I helped her take it off and hung it up.

After I hung up it up, I walked back over to her and she was about to say something but I didn't let her talk. Without even asking I just started tongue-kissing her. She seemed as if she didn't have a shy bone in her body, and she kissed me just as passionately as I kissed her.

I started unbuttoning her top as I kissed her, and before long her full thirty-six-D titties were exposed and I was sucking on them. I took off my shirt and she started feeling on my chest. She told me to sit on the bed and just lay back. I did as she instructed me, and she took off my sneakers and then unbuttoned my pants and pulled them off.

"That's sexy as hell."

"What?" I asked.

"You ain't wearing no underwear. I love that!"

After she said that, she took my dick and started sucking on it like a pro. She was driving me insane. Then she took my balls and started gently sucking on them while she stroked my dick with her hand. I could tell that she definitely had a whole lot of experience sucking dick and I can't say that I was mad at that because it was feeling good as hell.

"You got a condom?" she asked.

I nodded my head and told her where it was. She got up and went across the room and got the condom and then she took off her boots and squirmed her thick-ass body out of the tight jeans she had on. The only light that was coming into the room was the streetlights and the moonlight that was shining in through the window. But there was enough light for me to see that Mashonda had a body like a stripper.

She put the condom on my dick as I laid with my back on the bed. Then she stood over me and I know she did that just so I could see her entire body and her shaved pussy. As I held my dick, she slowly slid her pussy on top of it and worked her ass and thighs real slow until she had all of my dick inside of her.

She kept letting out these gasps of ecstasy each time she went up and down on my dick. Before long her pussy was soaking wet, so I grabbed her ass with both of my hands and I started to fuck the shit outta her. I could tell that she was really enjoying it just because of the yelling that she was doing.

"Yeah, grab my ass just like that!"

"You like that shit?"

"Yes! I love it!"

"You like getting fucked hard?"

"Emmmhh-hhmmmm! You are driving me crazy! Your dick feels so good. Urrrgggh!"

I stood up and I picked her up in the process, putting her on her back and pushing her legs all the way back and started fucking her as hard as I could.

"Oh, my God. Lance, you feel so fucking good! You gonna make me cum!"

I fucked her in that position for about five minutes and she came twice, real hard, and in the process she was ripping into my back with her nails but I didn't give a shit. All I was focused on was gettin' mines off.

I turned her around and started fucking her doggystyle, and just seeing all of her ass jiggling everywhere was incredible, and in no time I was ready to cum. I pulled my dick out of her and slid the condom off and I came all over her ass and her back.

"Wow! Wow! Wow!" I shouted as I plopped myself onto the bed next to her.

Mashonda giggled and she didn't say anything else. She just smiled at me and continued laying with her stomach on the bed.

"I see you're trying to make a nigga fall in love."

She smiled again but she didn't say anything. Then she got up and ran both of her hands down her face and walked into the bathroom. I could hear her running the water in the shower, so I got up and walked toward the bathroom.

"You bouncing?" I asked.

"No, I can chill. I'm just gonna take a quick shower."

"Okay. You gotta work tomorrow?"

"Yeah, but I don't have to be there until eight-thirty. So I can chill with you until like six."

It sounded like a plan to me because I definitely wanted to smash that one more time before the night was over.

I wanted to jump in the shower with her but I decided to just chill. I walked over to my phone and I saw that it was after one in the morning and I also noticed that I had three missed calls from Nicole. It wasn't until that moment that I felt like shit. I tried to figure out what I should do. I mean, I didn't want to call Nicole right at that moment because I didn't want to disrespect Mashonda like that. Plus Mashonda didn't even know I was married so I also needed some time to try and figure out how I was gonna break that news to her that's if I was going to break that news to her at all.

"Lance, what the fuck are you doing?" I asked myself.

The answer was I didn't know what the fuck I was doing. But as I turned my phone off and put it on the desk that was in my room, I did know that I had just done again what I had vowed over and over and over again not to repeat.

I was weak and I had slipped up once again, but there was no sense in beating myself up at that point. What was done was done. I had a sexy-ass, butt-naked, dime piece in the bathroom taking a shower and I knew that that was all I needed to focus on at the time.

It was all about Mashonda as far as I was concerned.

Chapter Four

Being that Philadelphia was only a two-hour drive from New York, the publishing company had provided all of the The Unit authors with a car service that chauffeured us individually back to New York in Lincoln town cars.

By the time I woke up, took a shower, got dressed, and ate breakfast with Mashonda it was after nine-thirty and I knew that I had to bounce ASAP. She had already called her job and told them that she would be late. As for me, I knew I needed to call Nicole and I was feeling guilty as shit, but I did my best to push those thoughts to the back of my head and not think about the guilt.

"So am I gonna see you again?" Mashonda asked. "Of course you will," I responded, but I wasn't 100 percent sure I meant what I was saying. Granted, Mashonda looked every bit as good on the morning after as she had the night before so that was a definite plus that she had in her favor. But I had hit it already so I wasn't sure if I even really wanted to be bothered with her anymore.

"Come here," I said as I reached out my hand and guided her closer to me. We had pulled the drapes fully closed so that the blinding sunlight wouldn't light up the room, so there was still this cozy feel as the television played in the background.

Mashonda pressed her body up against mines and we kissed each other for about a minute or so.

"Emmmh, you drive me so fucking crazy!" Mashonda said as she pulled away from me and smiled. "You sure you didn't slip nothing in my drink because I can't explain this shit."

I chuckled and shook my head *no* as I grabbed my bag and prepared to leave. Mashonda said what she had said because she knew that the only explanation for her actions was that she was a whore. And since she, like most women, never want to believe that they're a whore, tried to explain away her actions by making a joke about me slipping her a mickey.

"The car is downstairs waiting for me. So here, take this. Get you some gas for your car and pay for your parking with it, a'ight?" I said as I handed her one hundred dollars.

"Thank you. You're so sweet," she replied and gave me a kiss on my cheek as we stepped into the elevator.

With the way Mashonda took the money so easily I knew that she was a gold-digging whore. She was no different than the big-butt strippers who would leave the strip club and fuck a nigga as long as he was putting up cash for the pussy. Yeah, Mashonda knew what time it was and so did I, but I couldn't knock her hustle.

When we got to the lobby I immediately saw my driver and I headed toward him.

"Lance Thomas?"

"Yeah, yeah, that's me."

"Right this way," the driver replied as he directed me outside into the freezing cold and toward the car. He held the rear-passenger door open for me and just before I stepped into the car I turned and gave Mashonda a hug and a peck on the lips.

"It was real."

"Yeah, it was. Call me when you get back to New York."

"No doubt."

I sat into the plush leather seats, and the driver had already had the heat on so the car was very comfortable inside. But my mind wasn't at ease simply because I knew that I should have left Philly the night before and had my ass back in New York. I kept my cell phone turned off, because I knew that Nicole would be blowing my phone up to no end.

"Listen, here's sixty dollars. Do whatever you can to get me back to New York as quick as possible."

The Arab driver thanked me for the generous tip and told me that he would do his best. Then he proceeded to maneuver toward the Ben Franklin Bridge and eventually we ended up on the New Jersey Turnpike where I fell asleep and didn't wake up until we were in New York and on the Long Island Expressway.

It was a little after eleven in the morning and I knew that my son's game started at eleven, so instead of the driver taking me straight to my house I had him drop me at my son's school.

When I got to the school, I spoke to the security guard for a quick second and then I headed straight for the crowded gymnasium. As soon as I walked into the gym I could see that all of the seats in the bleachers were full so I decided to stand a few feet away from the entrance along with some of the other parents.

Apparently my son LL had just gotten fouled and he was standing at the free throw line preparing to shoot a foul shot.

"LL!" I shouted. "LL!"

Just as the referee handed LL the ball I managed to get his attention and I made a fist with my right hand and thumped it across my chest two times. That was the sign that I had made up for LL and whenever I did that he knew that it meant for him to go hard and to play with heart.

LL nodded his head to acknowledge me and then he bounced the ball three times, bent his knees, blew some air from his lungs, and took the shot and made it. He pointed in my direction before running back down the court to play defense.

"Man, that kid is really good!" one of the white parents standing next to me said.

"Yeah, that's my boy, Little Lance," I said with a huge, proud smile across my face. "I was hoping that I made it here on time. What quarter is this?"

"Oh, you just got here? It's the third quarter. Your son really put on a show in the first half, he's definitely on another level for a sixth grader."

Just as the guy said that, LL came down court and sank a three-point shot that forced the other team to call a time-out. After the time-out LL's coach left him on the bench and I know it was because he didn't want to embarrass the other team. LL's team was already up by twenty points and had he left LL in the game their lead only would have increased. But LL loved the game so much that he hated being on the bench, and you could see the anger in his eleven-year-old face.

"Hey, baby," Nicole said to me as she walked up to me and kissed me on the cheek.

"Nicole, you just got here?" I asked with a surprised tone.

"No, you just got here. I was sitting in the bleachers and I saw you when you walked in."

Right then and there I was bracing for the drama that I knew I was gonna get from Nicole for not having called her before I left Philly.

"Look at your son sitting all slumped and dejected looking. It is so embarrassing. You better talk to him about that. He's really gotta cut that out. It's so bratty!"

"Yeah, I will, as soon as he gets home today. Listen Nicole, I'm sorry I didn't call you but the battery in my phone died and I forgot my charger at the crib," I said in an attempt to preempt the barrage of questions that I knew she would hit me with for not having called her.

"At least I thought I forgot it. It wasn't until I was packing my stuff this morning, getting ready to leave, that I realized that my charger was in my back. It was just covered up by my pants."

Nicole laughed and replied, "Baby, it's okay, I'm not trippin'. As long as you're safe, I'm okay. I'm just glad you made it to his game because you know he would've had a fit if you didn't come."

I felt some relief that Nicole didn't grill me like I thought she would, and at the same time, more than anything, I realized that it was probably just my conscience making me feel guilty and causing me to expect the worst when I really had nothing to fear. Or at least that's what I thought.

What happened was after the game was over, LL continued on with his day at school and I went home and went to sleep. Nicole had told me that she was heading back to her office and that she wouldn't be home until about six-thirty that evening. But apparently she made it home much sooner.

"Lance, Lance, wake up," Nicole said as she shook me.

Although I felt like I had been sleeping for days, I groggily turned and looked at the clock and saw that it was only a little past two o'clock in the afternoon.

"Hey, baby, I thought you was going to the office?" I said, still half-asleep.

"Lance, sit up. Get up. We got a problem."

"What's wrong?" I asked, but I was too tired to sit up.

"This is what's wrong!" Nicole barked out as she threw something at me.

I felt something hit my face and that got me to finally sit up and pay attention.

"Lance, whatever you do, please don't lie to me! Just tell me the truth!"

"Ahhh shit!" I screamed out in my head as I saw a condom laying on the floor of my bedroom. That was what Nicole had thrown at me.

"Tell you the truth about what?" I asked, trying to play dumb.

"About that condom!"

"What condom? What are you talking about?"

"I'm talking about I came back home early to surprise you with a afternoon quickie. When I saw you sleeping I figured you were probably too tired to put your stuff away from your trip, so I was gonna put it away for you, and that's when I found a condom in your bag. And not three condoms or a box of condoms, I only found one condom, Lance! One condom! And since we don't use condoms, my question is, what was it doing in your bag? And better yet, what happened to the other condoms?" Nicole screamed. I knew she was heated.

All of a sudden I was wide awake and I knew I had to think quick.

"Nicole, I don't know where that came from or how it got there," I calmly said, trying my hardest to play things cool.

Nicole looked at me with twisted lips, and she shook her head.

"I don't! Why you giving me that look?"

"Lance, just tell me the truth!"

"I told you the truth! *I don't know where it came from!* I mean I don't know, Lameek or Fifth coulda put it there as a joke or something," I barked, as I was starting to get angry.

"So let's get them on the phone right now then," Nicole vented, calling my bluff.

My heart was pounding like crazy and I didn't need this shit, but I knew that I had forgotten my number-one rule about never being sloppy with shit. But there was no way in hell that I was gonna forget rule number two. I was not gonna admit to shit under no circumstances.

"Nicole, give me my phone!" I yelled as I got up and tried to retrieve my cell phone.

"No! Let's get Lameek and Fifth on the phone and ask them about this condom thing!" Nicole angrily yelled while scrolling through the phone book on my phone.

"Give me my phone! I'm not calling them with no bullshit like that. You know how stupid I would look?" I replied with both fear and anger.

Nicole sucked her teeth and then threw the phone at me with all her strength. The phone hit me and then fell to the ground.

"So you're more worried about how you would look in front of your boys than your wife?" Nicole shook her head. "Do you know how pathetic you sound right now?"

I couldn't have cared less how pathetic I sounded, but there was no way I was gonna call anybody and catch them off guard and make a bad situation worse. So I kept my mouth shut and bent down and picked up the phone.

"Okay, you know what, we don't have to call anybody, just give me your phone so I can check something," Nicole said calmly. She was calm but it was one of those clenched-teeth calm looks where she could have blew off the handle at any time.

"So you can check what?"

"I wanna check your phone, Lance! What is the problem?"

"The problem is, what happened to the trust, Nicole? It's been six years now, cut me some slack!"

"What happened to the trust? Trust is something that you have to earn!"

"So in six years I haven't earned it?"

"Lance, as much as this is about trust, this is also about openness and honesty."

"Whatever, but you ain't looking at my phone. I don't know what you gotta do, but Nicole, you need to get over this shit. It's been six years! Six years, Nicole! Niggas in the street kill people and they do less time than that!" I was acting angry and I was hoping that my reverse psychology would work.

"Oh, so you've been in prison, huh? Well, I tell you what, that phone in your hand can be your get out of jail free card because if you don't let me see it then you gotta get outta this house! And I mean that, Lance."

"Babe, you are really bugging out right now and overreacting."

"Lance, I been through this before, and I cannot go through this again."

I knew I hadn't deleted all of my texts from my phone and I still had all of my recent calls from the night before. Plus I didn't know if Mashonda had texted me or left me any voice mail messages while I had my phone turned off, so there was no way I was going to give Nicole that phone.

"Nicole, this is some bullshit!" I said as I started to put on my pants. "I'm gonna step out and get some food and when I come back home and when you come back home we need to just press the reset button and start over." That was the only thing I could think to do or say. It was either fight or flight. I knew the fight option would have been the wrong option so I just needed some time to think of my next move.

Nicole was quiet. She shook her head and started heading out of the bedroom and toward the downstairs steps. As she walked away I could hear her sobbing.

"What are you crying for, baby?"

"Lance, pack up your shit and get the fuck outta this house!" Nicole shouted as she stopped dead in her tracks. I knew that whenever my wife cursed that she was highly upset and was not playing games.

I caught up to her and put my arms around her. "Baby, please just—"

"Lance, get your hands off of me! Pack up your shit and get the fuck out!"

She flung herself free from me and continued on downstairs and she hollered the whole way down to the living room.

"You brought another child into this world by another woman and I stood by you! I did my part big time! You can't even begin to understand how hard it is to deal with something like that on an everyday basis and now you wanna just throw that up in my face like I'm supposed to just get over it? No, I don't need to get over anything but your black ass and your bullshit. You quit your job a few years ago to follow your dream as a writer, and I overlooked my reservations about that because I didn't want to be selfish, but this is the exact reason why I knew you writing and getting into that career wasn't a good idea. But did I hold you back? No, I didn't and this is the thanks I get, right? You got some serious problems, Lance. You need to get help and work out those problems, but you just gonna have to work it out outside of this house because I'm telling you right now that you are not staying here."

I went back into my room and quickly turned my phone on and it seemed like it was taking forever to turn on.

"Hurry up!" I pleaded with the phone until it finally came on. I knew that after all Nicole had just said that I couldn't just turn away and run to my room the second that she was done talking. It would have come across as crazy disrespectful, but I had to get rid of any incriminating evidence.

I feverishly started deleting all of my old text messages but new texts were coming in just as fast as I was deleting the old texts. Finally, after five minutes I had deleted all of the texts and my recent call log of any remotely incriminating phone calls that I had made or received. I wanted to check my voice mail but I knew that I didn't have that kind of time, so I took my chances without listening to the voice mail messages, and I ran downstairs to Nicole.

"Baby, here, you want my phone, take it," I said as I threw the phone on to the granite kitchen countertop. "This is really a waste of time but if this is gonna make you feel more comfortable, then look through the phone, I don't care. All I know is this is gonna set us back like the whole six years that we been rebuilding." I said that in an attempt to deflect attention from myself. I was a master at causing problems and then painting myself as the victim.

Nicole was still slightly sobbing and she didn't initially say anything nor did she make a move for my phone. Then after about a minute or so she wiped the tears from her face and she calmly began to talk and said, "Lance, you know the truth. You know why you didn't answer my calls last night. You know why you didn't call me back. You know why there was a condom in your bag, and you know why you didn't want me to look at your phone until *after* you deleted what you wanted to delete. Yup, you know all of that and all of the details. I may not know all of the details that you know, and to be honest I don't wanna know all of the details, but I do know what I know, Lance, and it's time for you to get your things and go."

"Baby—"

"Lance, just go!" Nicole yelled and gave me this look to kill.

I shook my head and blew some air from my lungs and calmly headed back up to my room. I sat on my bed for a couple of minutes thinking how I had really just fucked up but I also trying to think of a way to make things right. I knew that Nicole wasn't playing games and that I had to quickly get my shit and get the hell out of Dodge.

Chapter Five

Steve had been my right-hand man for as long as I could remember. Whenever I was in a crisis situation he was usually the first person that I would reach out to. And with Nicole putting me out of the house, I definitely was in a crisis situation. But as I figured he would, Steve took me in with open arms.

"So my nigga is putting his jersey back on! Ha-ha! Yeah, baby! That's what I'm talking about."

"Steve, this is serious, man. Nicole ain't playing this time."

Steve made his way to the bar in his dining room and poured us both a glass of Hennessy. He didn't mix it with soda nor did he put any ice in it.

"Drink that. Just gulp it down. Don't sip that shit."

I listened to Steve and I drank the Hennessy as he instructed and he did the same.

"See, that's grown-man shit right there. Here, drink some more of this shit," he said as he poured some more liquor in my glass.

"Listen, Lance, you my man, so you know I can tell you what's up without you trippin'. And what the problem witchu is that you was in retirement and you came outta retirement on a whim. You came out all rusty and shit and you fucked up! That's all that happened; nothing more, nothing less. But the main thing is your ass is back in the game, you feel me?"

Steve was always gonna be Steve and he wasn't gonna change or conform for nobody, so I had to respect him for that. At the same time, it didn't make sense for me to try and get him to understand any of the guilt or anxiety I was feeling because he wouldn't have been able to process it.

"So Mashonda is off the chain? Fill a nigga in!"

I was starting to feel the effects of the alcohol and I had a nice buzz.

"Whaaaat? Yo, her body is sick! She's a young, tender twenty-year-old thing, so you know it was bananas! And she looks good as hell too."

"Say word! She's only twenty?"

"Yeah, I mean when I first saw her I was thinking she was like twenty-seven or twenty-eight, but she showed me her license and she's only twenty years old, and her body is tight as hell even after one baby. The stomach is still flat and her titties are still standing up."

"So you saying you met the chick in the bank, invited her to the book signing and the release party and hit it the same night? Yo, my ass needs to start writing fucking books! That shit is crazy."

"It's that The Unit affiliation. That's what she's seeing, and that's what got her open like that," I explained.

"So the hell what! Play that shit up to your advantage. Matter of fact, take my ass witchu to the next book shit that you got going on so some of this shit can rub off on my ass," Steve said with a laugh.

Me and Steve continued to drink Hennessy and get drunk with each other. The more he drank the more foolishness he spoke and the more of a negative influence he became.

"Lance, you ain't ready to die, right?"

I looked at him and just shook my head *no* as I tried to figure out where he was gonna go with his statement.

"'Cause you know what they say about a dog that tastes blood. After he tastes blood you either gotta kill his ass or let him loose to go wild and do his thing. You tasted blood with Mashonda, and since you ain't ready to be put down it's time to turn your ass loose!"

As soon as Steve was done talking, my cell phone rang and I saw that it was Mashonda. I started to let her go to voice mail because I really didn't want to be bothered at all. But I picked up anyway.

"What's up, sexy?"

I could tell that Mashonda was cheesing through the phone.

"Nothing. I'm just checking up on you. I just got off work so I was seeing what you're up to. Did you get my message I left you?"

"Nah, I didn't even check my messages yet. I got back and went to sleep so I was really in chill mode."

"Oh, okay, so that's what's up. But listen, I was thinking about coming up there this weekend to see you."

Oh, hell no! I remember initially thinking to myself. If there was one thing I didn't need, it was for Mashonda to become a bug-a-boo. And she was already showing the signs of a bug-a-boo, blowing up my phone with messages and now she was asking to come check me.

I was sure that Mashonda had picked up on my hesitation and she jumped right in to break up the awkwardness.

"Well, I mean I got family in New York, so I was gonna come see them and then I was hoping that we could see each other again," she added.

"Yeah, okay, definitely. Just let me know if it's definite or not and we'll link up. So where does your family live, what part of New York?"

"Oh, well, the majority of them are in Harlem. What about you, where do you stay?"

"In Great Neck, out on Long Island, but—"

"Oh, so you a baller for real," she added with a little chuckle.

Steve was signaling for me to hang up the phone and waving his hands back and forth across his throat.

"Listen, Mashonda, let me hit you back later on, okay?"

"Okay, baby, no problem. Just make sure you call me," she said before we both hung up.

"That was the Philly chick?" Steve asked.

I nodded my head that it was as I got up and poured me another drink.

"Yo, Lance, you already smashed that. What the fuck are you making love on the phone with her for now? Stick and move nigga, stick and move. And why the hell are you telling her where you rest at?"

"Good pussy will make a nigga do anything!" I replied.

Steve looked at me and tapped my drink with his, and he chuckled.

"Yo, since your ass like to make love on the phone, I got somebody that I want you to speak to," Steve said as he dialed a number on his cell phone and handed it to me.

"Who the fuck is this?"

"Just talk, nigga!"

I looked at Steve's cell phone and I could see the name that he had dialed: Layla.

A big smile came across my face as Layla picked up.

"Hey, Steve," she said, obviously expecting it to be Steve since it was his number that was calling her.

"What's up, Layla? This ain't Steve, this is Lance," I responded.

"Lance? Oh my God! What's up? How are you?" She was obviously glad to hear from me.

As the night would play itself out, I was gonna find out that not only was I gonna be glad to hear from her, but I was also going to find out that Steve was right about a dog getting that taste of blood. See, because with me, Mashonda had been that taste of blood, and I was ready to let loose and like a crazed dog in heat I wanted to taste some more blood and now I had my sights set on Layla.

Again, I was using that unique ability that I was not proud of, to shift my feelings of guilt and thoughts of love for my wife to one side of my brain. By doing that I was able to operate as if I had no conscience at all.

Chapter Six

I had been at Steve's house less than two hours and within that time I was drunk out of my mind. I had basically invited myself over to Layla's house in Brooklyn where she lived with her teenage daughter and an eleven-year-old daughter, both by different fathers.

Before heading over to Layla's house, I took a shower at Steve's crib and changed my clothes and got real fly. My one-night-stand experience with Mashonda had taught me that all I had to do was walk with the expectation of getting pussy, maintain a certain confidence, and know that I could get any woman to take her panties of for me regardless of how long I knew the woman or how close we were. The key for me was not to come across desperate to fuck or needy and like a crack-head needing a hit of crack. So when I arrived at her house, which was in Canarsie, I maintained that same sense of confidence even through my drunkenness.

"Lance!" Layla replied with a big smile and a hug as she greeted me at the door. "I see you been hitting the weights or something, you look so good."

Layla and I had only met once about a year ago at a Super Bowl party that Steve had at his crib. We had chilled with each other and kicked it the whole night of the Super Bowl and although we had exchanged numbers I never pushed up on her, nor did I feed into her advances when she would call me, because I was trying my best to stay focused. But that was then and this was now, and all I was concerned with was now.

"That hug felt good. Come here, give me another one," I said as I grabbed her and pressed my body up against hers.

Then we separated and just stared at each other for a moment before Layla smiled and asked me to stop staring at her.

"You know who you look like?"

"Yeah, I know, the actress Lauren London who played in the movie *This Christmas,*" she replied as if she had been told that a million times.

"Nah, but really, you do. I mean, you're sexier than she is, but you still look like her."

"Whatever, she's younger than me so she looks like me," Layla joked.

She invited me in to see the rest of her house and asked me if she could take me on a quick tour of her place. Of course I didn't mind, so I followed her around as she took me from room to room. In the process she introduced me to her daughters. They both were cute and looked just like their mother.

Layla was renting one half of a two-family house. She had three bedrooms, a living room, a dining room, a nice kitchen, and two bathrooms, and she kept the place immaculate, and it was well-decorated.

"And this is my room, my little oasis," she said, smiling as she opened the door to her room.

"Is that ocean sounds?" I asked.

Layla nodded her head *yes* and explained that she kept that ocean sounds CD playing all day long because it helped relax her and instantly removed any stress that she might be feeling.

"That's different, I like that," I said as I took hold of her hand. "This takes away stress too," I said and without asking I leaned in and started tongue-kissing her. And without any resistance she began kissing me back. She was really getting into it as she hugged me as tight as she could and kissed me as hard as she could for about two minutes straight.

"Whoa, whew," Layla said as she shook her head and smiled and stepped away from me. "I definitely didn't see that one coming."

I didn't say anything. I just looked at her.

"Um, yeah, we need to go into the kitchen or the living room or somewhere, anywhere but here," she said to me as she headed out of her room. Layla was walking in her bare feet and she was wearing what looked like a large head scarf with some kind of African print on it that she was using as a body wrap.

"You want something to eat?" she asked as she walked in front of me with her ass looking sexy as hell in that wrap thing she was wearing.

I was starving, so I took her up on her offer. She sat me down at her dining room table. The next thing I knew I had a full plate of food in front of me: baked macaroni and cheese, candied yams, collard greens, fried chicken, and cornbread.

"Damn, you cooked all of this?"

"I love to cook, this is everyday for me," Layla explained as she got a bottle of red wine and filled a glass for me. She sat Indian-style in the chair that was directly across from mine. While I ate she looked at me and seemed to be enjoying the fact that I was enjoying her food, and then she took out a bunch of papers and turned on her laptop and started typing some stuff.

"What are you doing?"

"Just working on this case I gotta finish by tomorrow."

"What kind of case? What do you do again?"

Layla explained that she worked from home, and that she had her own business where she provided freelance paralegal services to immigration lawyers and attorneys who handled accident cases.

I nodded my head and told her that I was impressed.

"You know you breaking all the light-skin girl stereotypes, right? I mean, you can cook your ass off, and you got a head on your shoulders, and a nice ass and nice titties! You're three for three!"

"Boy, I will stab you with that fork! No, you didn't just say that," she said while she laughed at me.

"I'm saying, you know I'm right. Pretty, light-skin chicks usually have either a fat butt or big titties, not both. And I have yet to meet one that can put their foot in some food like you did with this food."

Layla just shook her head and smiled.

As I ate we started talking about everything. She complained to no end about her deadbeat ex-husband and I untruthfully told her about my issues with Nicole. Before long it was approaching ten-thirty and we were sitting on her living room couch watching a movie with all of the lights off. Somehow my hand made its way underneath that wrap thing that she was wearing, and I eventually located her pussy and started rubbing on it. Right from the first touch I noticed that she was soaking wet.

"Lance, I love the way you touch me," she purred with her eyes closed.

I continued to finger-fuck her and her pussy continued to get wetter by the second. As she gyrated her hips I pulled her wrap all the way up so that her pussy was fully exposed. Since I had drank a whole bottle of wine, which was combined with the Hennessy that I had from earlier, I was feeling so intoxicated that I didn't give a shit about anything. So the next thing I knew, my bald head was in Layla's crotch and I was eating her pussy for dessert.

I sucked on her clit while I slid my index finger in and out of her pussy, and within seconds Layla was grabbing my head and squeezing it as she gyrated her hips and came hard as hell. I was shocked that she was just letting herself go like that. I mean, she was hollering like a porn star while she was cumming, and it was all good but she also had her two daughters in the other room, which was all of twenty feet away from where we were sitting.

I sat up to get some air and I looked at Layla and she was breathing really heavy and panting as she said, "I swear to God, ain't nobody ever make me cum that quick in my fucking life! Shit!"

I chuckled, and then I told her that we had to stop since her daughters were right there in the other room and could hear us.

"They'll be okay, don't worry about that," she said to me as she stood up and straightened out her clothes. "You eat my pussy like that, you know you gotta fuck me now," she added rather matter-of-factly.

"Where at? We can't do that right here," I said, trying not to talk too loud.

The next thing I know Layla had untied her wrap and her naked body was fully exposed. She opened her legs and spread her pussy lips apart, just inviting me to come fuck her.

I was drunk but I wasn't crazy. There was no way I was gonna fuck Layla right there on her living room couch and get busted by her daughters. They didn't need to see nothing like that. So I grabbed Layla by her hand and led her to her bedroom and closed the door.

"Please tell me you got a condom," I said to her.

"I got you, don't worry about that," she said as she took my shirt off and kissed on my chest while unbuckling my pants. "Layla, I'm not fucking you raw!"

Layla didn't respond, she just looked up at me and held her index finger to her mouth and went to the other side of her room. When she came back, she started sucking on my dick, and while both of our hands were interlocked with each other's, she managed to put a condom on my dick by using her mouth and nothing else.

"Oh shit, where the fuck you learn that?" I asked.

Layla didn't answer me, she just got on her bed and she was on all fours waiting for me to get behind her and fuck her and that was exactly what I did. I pushed her head into the mattress so that her face was down and her ass was up in the air and I wore her ass out doggystyle.

She tried her best to keep quiet while she bit into one of her pillows, but every time she came she would let the whole fucking neighborhood know that she was cumming. I know that her kids had to hear everything that was going on because the house was basically quiet, and they were in the bed since it was a school night.

"I wanna feel that shit on my face when you cum. Okay, baby?" she turned and said to me while I fucked her.

I nodded my head and kept fucking her as hard as I could until I felt myself ready to erupt.

"Ahhh yeah, it's cumming, baby!" I said as I pulled out of her pussy and quickly took the condom off.

Layla turned around and laid on her back and then quickly scooted herself closer toward me so that her face was right near my balls. When I bussed I came all over her face, in her hair, and in her mouth.

She smiled as she licked some of my cum with her tongue and played with it in her mouth before spitting it back out.

I sat up on her bed and caught my breath. As I contemplated whether I should spend the night with her or go back to Steve's house, I realized that I was living totally out of control. But at the same time I really didn't give a shit. I was who I was and I was doing me. The way I was living was in my DNA since birth, and I was starting to love every minute of my lifestyle that was quickly spiraling out of control.

The first time I had cheated on Nicole I battled continuously with guilt and trying to do what was right for her and trying to do right by God. But it was like I was at the point now where I was saying to myself that it was pathetic to constantly be sitting on the fence. I knew that I had to either shit or get off of the pot. And getting off of the pot to me meant getting a divorce. But regardless of my actions, which seemed to prove otherwise, I still loved my wife and my son a great deal. Therefore, I knew that my only option was to stay on the pot and shit. Even if I was shitting on myself I was cool with that because there was just no way I was going to stay in that same wishy-washy state of mind of trying to do right and burning to do wrong.

Chapter Seven

The next morning when I woke up, I was feeling hung-over and I had no idea where I was until Layla came into her bedroom with breakfast for me.

"What time is it?"

"It's nine-fifteen," she replied as she handed me a tray full of food. "Layla, you didn't have to do this."

"I know, but I wanted to do it. I told you I love to cook.

When people come to my house, they eat. I take care of everybody that walks through my door."

Layla was really no joke. She knew exactly how to treat a nigga and she pushed all the right buttons. She had made cheese grits, bacon, scrambled eggs, and French toast. And not only had she made breakfast for me, but she had also washed, dried, and ironed the clothes that I had on from the day before.

"When the hell did you do all of this?"

Layla didn't respond directly to my question. She just smiled and told me to take my time eating and that she was going to finish up that case that she had been working on from the night before.

"I put a towel, soap, lotion, a brand new tooth-brush for you in the bathroom when you're ready to get dressed. The girls already left for school so just feel at home. Okay?"

I smiled and thanked her. As I ate the food that she had cooked for me, I couldn't help but think about how Nicole used to treat me this good way back when we had first gotten married. But unfortunately for me and Nicole, life got in the way and all of the pampering that I used to get just disappeared along with the sex. So by nature Layla was scoring big points as far as I was concerned.

As I ate and then prepared to take a shower and get dressed, I would be lying if I said that I wasn't feeling deeply conflicted. Because on one hand I wanted to snatch up Layla and fuck the shit out of her again, and on the other hand I wanted to see my wife and make love to her and tell her that I was sorry for screwing up. Yet the thing that was troubling me the most was that I knew that my son was probably wondering why I hadn't spoken to him since his game.

I knew what I needed to do. After I had taken my shower and gotten dressed, I thanked Layla for treating me like a king and for showing me an amazing time. I kissed her on the lips and told her that I really had to bounce.

"You sure you don't wanna stay?"

"I want to, but I really got moves that I need to make."

"Okay, so listen. I hope it's not gonna be a whole year before I hear from you again or see you again."

I shook my head and explained to her that she had a license to call me and see me whenever she wanted to, and that I would get up with her in a few days.

"Yeah, we gotta hang out real soon," she said to me.

"Definitely," I replied as I kissed her again on her lips before walking out the door.

I jumped in my all black Range Rover and headed straight for my son's school. When I got there I headed straight for the principal's office and explained that it was an emergency and that I really needed to speak to my son for a few minutes.

The lady in the principal's office was very sweet and accommodating. She told me to have a seat and she would handle everything. She got on the phone and within about three minutes or so my son walked into the principal's office.

"Daddy!" he said with a big smile. Because of the expression on his face I know that he was shocked to see me.

"What's up, homie?" I said to him as I held out my hand for him to slap me five.

I then took LL by the hand and walked him into the hallway so that we could talk in private.

"You okay?"

He nodded his head and told me that he was fine.

"Listen, I just wanted to tell you that I didn't come home last night because I still have to promote this new book so I'm gonna be out of town for a few days, okay?"

"You're gonna be with Fifth Ward?" LL smiled and asked. He thought that was the coolest thing, that his dad had written a book with a rap icon.

"Well, he's real busy so he's not gonna be with me for the whole time."

"So when will you be back?"

"I'm not sure, but I'll make sure I call you every day, okay?"

LL nodded.

"And listen, you played real good the other day but what was that stunt you pulled when the coach took you outta the game?"

LL turned up his lips and a frown came on his face as he explained, "I was playing real good and he shouldn't have taken me out. If I messed up then he should put me on the bench, not when I'm playing good and doing everything right!"

"But LL, y'all were blowing the other team out."

"So?"

"So, the right thing to do was to take you out so that y'all wouldn't embarrass the other team."

LL just shook his head because he totally didn't agree with me but he knew not to argue.

"Daddy, did you see that move I did when I crossed over on that white boy and he fell to the ground?" LL asked in an animated fashion.

I couldn't help but laugh at how amped and hyped he got when he spoke about basketball. It was like he was a completely different person because normally he was reserved and somewhat shy, but when it came to sports he was passionate as ever.

"I missed that. I got here too late but I'll see the videotape when they make it available to purchase. But listen, I just wanted to see you be-

fore I left. Make sure you knock out your home-
work and be good in school, okay? You can't
make it to the NBA if your grades aren't on point,
remember that."

LL looked at me and nodded his head and
then he held out his fist for a pound. "So you're
out?"

I chuckled at him because he was always trying to be so cool, and you couldn't tell him that
he didn't have an eleven-year-old swagger.

"Yeah, I'm out. So go back to your classroom
and remember, call me whenever you want. I
don't care how early or how late it is, okay?"

"Okay," he replied and then walked off back to
his classroom

After seeing my son, I was good. If anything,
I knew that for my son's sake I had to straighten
up and do the right thing. But it still wasn't that
easy to do right.

I decided to shoot back to my crib and see
what was up with Nicole, because this getting
kicked out of the house shit was crazy, and I
figured that after she had some time to calm
down she would see things differently.

Apparently, though, when I reached my crib
I realized that Nicole was really going hard
body! She literally had all of the locks to the crib
changed.

"Yo, this is some bullshit!" I yelled as I began banging on the front door and ringing the bell like I had lost my mind.

"Nicole, open the goddamn door!"

I banged on the front door, the side door, and the back door for about five minutes and I got no answer. I realized that Nicole must have left for work. So with my blood boiling, I hopped back in my truck and made it from Great Neck, Long Island to Rosedale, Queens in like five minutes when it normally takes about fifteen.

Nicole rented an office suite that was located inside of an office complex called Cross Island Plaza. It was a nice building located on Merrick Boulevard and it had pretty good security. Since I was always coming there, security already knew me so they never made me sign and never called Nicole's suite to announce that I was there to see her.

So I said, "What's up?" to the security guards and I kept it moving. Nicole was on the third floor but I didn't waste any time waiting on the elevator. I stormed up the steps and into Nicole's suite.

"Hey, Becky, where's Nicole?" I asked Nicole's blond-haired, blue-eyed secretary.

"Oh, hi, Lance, she's actually meeting with someone."

I totally tuned the secretary out and I went straight for Nicole's office and she wasn't there, so I knew that she had to be inside the conference room.

"Um, excuse me, Lance, but she's really in an important meeting. I think you should wait until she's done."

I ignored her and without knocking I walked right into the conference room where I saw Nicole sitting at the table with a legal notepad and she was writing something down. The paralegal was there and there were two other people in the room, a white dude and a black lady, both of who looked like they were in their late forties or early fifties.

"Nicole, can I talk to you for a second," I said with a stern tone in my voice.

I was dressed in my Timbs, jeans, a dark blue leather bomber vest, and a hooded sweatshirt, and when Nicole looked up and saw me I could feel the fire coming from her. She had a look that said she wanted to kill.

"I'm so sorry, can everyone please excuse me for a moment," she said as she got up and brushed past me and headed straight for her office with me following behind her. When we made it into her office she made sure the door was shut and then she turned to me and with her teeth clenched she said, "God help you if you're not here to tell me that something happened to my son!"

"Nicole, how the hell you change the fucking locks!" I shouted.

"Would you keep your voice down! What is wrong with you? I'm meeting with an important client."

I saw Nicole's pocketbook sitting on her desk and I went straight for it.

"You gonna give me those goddamn keys! There ain't no way in the world I'm gonna pay a bank eight thousand a month and can't live in my own shit!" I barked as Nicole ran up to me and snatched her pocketbook away from me.

"Nicole, I swear to God I will turn this whole office upside down if you don't give me those keys!"

"Lance, you ain't staying there, I'm not dealing with this no more. Now leave or I'm calling the police."

"Calling the police for what?"

"To lock your ass up if you don't leave."

"Oh, you wanna call the police? A'ight, so that's where you wanna take it?" I yelled. I don't ever remember being as mad as I was at that point and with rage running throughout my body I went to the front of Nicole's desk and squatted down and reached both of my hands underneath her desk. After I had a good grip I used all of my might and literally flipped her desk upside down, causing papers and shit to fly everywhere.

"Becky, Becky, call the police for me! Lance done lost his mind!" Nicole opened the door to her office and shouted out to Becky.

Becky came running to the office, not sure exactly what was going on and she saw me and Nicole tussling for her pocketbook.

"Becky, call 911!" Nicole screamed and Becky ran out of the office and picked up her phone and began dialing the cops.

"Let the bag go and I'll leave," I said to Nicole, who all of a sudden had a tremendous amount of strength.

At that point I heard the door to her conference room open, and I could hear the white guy asking her paralegal if I was one of Nicole's criminal clients. Nicole must have heard the same thing because at that point she loosened her grip on the pocketbook and told me to leave.

I looked at her. Her hair was a mess and her clothes were disheveled and her office looked like a tornado had hit it. But I didn't give a shit, I meant exactly what I said earlier about there being no way I was gonna pay eight thousand a month in mortgage payments and not be able to live in the house. That was absolutely crazy to me.

I stormed out of the building and I headed home to my truck, and as I let it warm up a bit, I began to calm down. I realized at that moment that I might have taken things just a bit too far. After a couple of minutes I put my truck in drive and maneuvered my way out of the parking lot. While I was handing money to the parking lot clerk, I looked over and saw Nicole coming out of the office building with two police officers. All I could do was shake my head because Nicole didn't even have to take things to that level, but I knew that she was probably gonna get a order of protection against me or some other type of spiteful shit.

Right after the clerk handed me my change I could hear someone yelling. I turned and looked and I saw Nicole pointing in the direction of my truck and the cops were quickly approaching my car.

"Can you lift the gate please?" I asked as my heart rate picked up.

"Hold it, hold it, hold it!" I heard a voice holler, and the next thing I knew there were two cops were at my truck. One was on the driver's side and the other one was on the passenger side, and they both had their guns drawn.

The cop on my side yanked open the driver's door and snatched me out of the truck and slammed me onto the cold concrete. Within seconds my hands were handcuffed behind my back and my face was inches away from a pile of snow that hadn't yet melted from days before.

"Ma'am, is that your pocketbook?" one of the cops asked Nicole.

Apparently she said that it was but I couldn't actually see her from my facedown position. But I was able to see the three other cop cars that had arrived in the parking lot. This whole thing was unfolding into way too much drama for absolutely nothing.

"Sir, do you have any weapons or any drugs on your possession?" the cop asked me, but out of anger I kept my mouth shut and didn't respond to his question, and I soon felt the cops thoroughly frisking me. After about two minutes more of laying on the cold ground, they helped me to my feet and stood me next to one of the police cars as they searched my truck.

By this point it seemed as if every office worker in the building was standing in the parking lot watching what was going on.

"A'ight, Nicole, you win! Now can you tell them to take these handcuffs off of me and let's end this bullshit?" I said to Nicole, who was still visibly angry.

She looked at me and walked away. The next thing I knew the cops had placed me under arrest and were reading me my rights and had placed me in the backseat of the police car. I couldn't believe that I had been arrested, but by the time I got to the precinct and had my mug shot taken and was fingerprinted, it didn't take much more for me to realize that this arrest was really real.

But it really hit home for me when I sat in the cell at the precinct and thought about the charges that I had been hit with: robbery, assault, disorderly conduct, and trespassing.

Ain't this a bitch? I thought to myself as I sat slumped on the metal bench inside the pissy jail cell.

Chapter Eight

There's a saying: *Hurt People, Hurt People.* The saying basically means that when someone is hurt in an emotional way by someone else, they will go out of their way to hurt the person who hurt them. Nicole was obviously feeling hurt by all of my actions and she really was trying to hurt my ass.

It was evident that she was trying to hurt me, because although I had been hit with some serious charges, those charges really had no substance to them, considering that we were still husband and wife. But yet Nicole had a bunch of connections with the Queens County district attorney's office and with one phone call she was able to get my case buried among the other cases. So what she was able to do with that phone call was to delay my seeing the judge.

I had been arrested on Thursday morning, and under most circumstances I would have seen a judge by Friday morning and either been released on my own recognizance or given a bail. I only would have been kept in jail if I couldn't make bail. But it was now Monday morning and I was just getting ready to see a fucking judge! And that was only because I had called Layla and she was able to work some of her attorney contacts who also had friends in the district attorney's office.

In addition to getting my case buried, Nicole had also tapped some of her news organization sources and with one phone call on Thursday afternoon I had instantly become an infamous figure. And that was because my face was on the front cover of Friday's edition of the *New York Daily News*. I knew that Nicole had to be behind the sensationalism of the story simply because of the way they connected me to Fifth Ward and The Unit. Her goal was to embarrass me and to hurt me like I'd hurt her. And I must say that she definitely landed some good knockout punches.

The headline in Friday's paper read: MEMBER OF THE UNIT JAILED FOR ROBBERY AND ASSAULT.

Underneath the headline was a picture of my mug shot that the police had taken of me inside the police precinct. The story went on to say how I was linked with Fifth Ward and how apparently the violence that followed him was now infecting the literary world. And it went on and on and on about things that were not even true, all for the sake of selling newspapers and making things bigger than it really was.

So being that the news organizations now had ahold of this story, the district attorney had to go hard on me and they were pushing the judge to set a high-ass bail. The judge folded under the pressure and hit me with a fifty thousand dollar bail, which was excessive considering the nature of my crime and considering that I had no prior felony arrest record.

My lawyer stood with me before the judge and informed the judge that I was prepared to make bail. The judge stated more legal talk and then he asked me if I understood the seriousness of what I had been charged with. After I told him that I did, my lawyer Victor Spitz, spoke up and said something to the judge, who then noted something on some papers that were in front of him before informing everyone of my next scheduled court appearance. And with that, I was finally free to go.

"Thank you for everything," I said to my lawyer as he packed up his things and we prepared to leave the courtroom.

Steve walked up to me and Attorney Spitz as we were walking out of the courtroom and gave me a pound and a quick ghetto embrace.

"There's gonna be a zoo outside with the media," Victor said to me. "Just try not to say anything specific about the details of what happened on Thursday between you and Nicole."

"Nah, I won't say anything. I'll let you handle that part."

Just before we got outside of the courthouse, my lawyer stopped so that we could talk for a moment. He reassured me that this was all bullshit and that it would go away.

"The district attorney will throw out the robbery and assault charges and you'll plead guilty to the two misdemeanors of trespassing and disorderly conduct, and that will be it. This whole thing will be treated no different than getting caught driving with a suspended license. But I gotta warn you, keep your nose clean. Do what you gotta do to work out a healthy situation with Nicole. If you violate the order of protection, you will be spending some time on Rikers Island."

I nodded my head and told Victor that I understood and I would be sure to watch my temper and stay in line. I also told him that I would follow up with him on Wednesday after I had some time to rest and to clear my head.

After we had taken care of that small talk, we walked out to the courthouse steps that were facing Queens Boulevard. There were a bunch of photographers, cameramen, and newspeople that rushed me, my lawyer, and Steve. They converged on the three of us and started asking all kinds of crazy questions at the same time.

"Lance, were you also a small-time crack dealer in the nineties like Fifth Ward?"

"The stories that you write, are any of them based on real life?"

I couldn't help but chuckle at the ignorant questions, and I just had to answer. At the same time, I knew that I had to play up the moment to my benefit. It paid to be controversial.

"Why couldn't I have been a drug kingpin? I think big, but I guess you're insinuating that I'm a small-fry. And to answer your question, Miss, I write fiction but I draw from real life."

"Oh, so are you saying you are a former drug dealer?"

I smiled and responded, "I didn't say that. You did."

"Why would you stoop to robbing your wife? Do you have a drug problem, Mr. Thomas?"

My lawyer butted in. "Mr. Thomas doesn't have a drug problem and the charges against him are frivolous. This was nothing more than a big misunderstanding."

I hadn't brushed my teeth or washed my ass in like five days, so I was desperately wanting to get to a shower and to a bed so I could get some real much needed sleep.

As we tried our best to make our way to our cars, a reporter shouted and asked me if there was anything that I wanted to say.

So I paused, smiled, and said, "Yeah, I just want everybody to know that my new book is called *Harlem Heat*. It hit the stores last Tuesday, so go check it out."

If I was gonna go through this bullshit I figured that I might as well profit from the publicity.

"What is it called?" the reporter asked as she jotted down notes.

"*Harlem Heat*," I replied.

Finally me and Steve were able to make it to his car. Just as we were about to get in, a van pulled up and sort of boxed us in. A lady got out of the passenger's side. She came over to my side of the car and tapped on the window.

I rolled the window down and she introduced herself as Meagan Washington.

"You look familiar," I said to her as I tried my hardest to figure out where I knew her from.

Then she handed me her card and that's when it hit me. She was an on-air television personality for this show on CBS called *Media Edition*. The show was similar to *Entertainment Tonight* and BET's *Black Carpet*.

"Meagan Washington, you look a little different with the coat and the winter hat," I explained with a smile.

She smiled and then told me that she would love to sit down with me and interview me for an upcoming episode of the show.

I was about to say something flirtatious to Meagan but I kept my cool and professional. I told her that I would love to be on her show.

"Do you have a cell phone on you? Let me give you my cell phone so we won't play phone tag or anything like that."

"Okay, sure," she replied as she took out her cell phone and removed the gloves from her hands and programmed my number as I read it off to her. "I'm gonna call you right now, lock my number in your phone too," she added.

Unfortunately, my cell phone was still at the police precinct along with my money and my wallet. So I had to explain to Meagan that the police still had it.

"Oh, okay," she said with a small chuckle and a smile.

Meagan extended her hand to me for a handshake, and I extended mine back.

"Nice meeting you. So we'll be in touch," she said before walking back to the black van with dark tinted windows.

As soon as she was back in the van and we were about to pull off, I said to Steve, "Yo, if meeting her was the reason that I got locked up, then there is no way I could be upset!"

"Lance, that's the major leagues right there, son!"

"Yup, and I'm a pro at this. I guarantee you I'll be smashing that soon," I said as I reclined my seat all the way back and just beamed from the thought of what it would be like to get with a chick on Meagan's level.

I knew that I had the power to do more than just imagine what it would be like to bag Meagan. I had the power to make bagging her a reality. And I was determined to do just that.

Chapter Nine

By the next day, Tuesday, I had managed to return the numerous amount of phone calls that I had received from people who had seen the news and were checking up on me just to see if I was all right.

My agent had called me, my editor had called, Fifth called, Mashonda called, Layla called, my sister called, my moms had called, all of the authors that I was cool with had called me. It was crazy. One by one I had managed to call everybody back and I made sure to make note of everybody who had chosen not to reach out to me. I did this because I wanted to take note of who was really riding with me and who I would have to remove from my life once this whole ordeal was behind me. Most notably, out of all people, I was surprised that Toni hadn't called.

I mean, I knew that she had long since moved on and was in a different space from the space that we had occupied when I was cheating with her. But I still had a five-year-old daughter by her and just on the strength of our daughter—whose name was Sahara—she could have called me. It was all good, though. Toni was living the good life with her super-successful husband and she was always coming across as if she didn't have the time of day for anybody. But I was sure that eventually the bad karma that she was throwing off would catch up to her and smack her ass with a dose of humble reality.

Around eight-thirty in the evening, my cell phone rang, and it was Nicole calling me from her cell phone. I had to think twice about picking up, because I didn't want to later have to deal with any okey-doke bullshit.

"Nicole, you're calling me, so I don't wanna hear no shit about me violating this stupid order of protection you got," I said as I answered the phone.

"Lance, I know that. But listen, LL got suspended from school today because apparently somebody called you a jailbird, and he didn't like that, so LL jumped on the kid and beat him down."

I shook my head and blew a whole lot of air into the phone. It took everything inside of me to restrain myself from flipping out on Nicole because this whole episode with LL could have easily been avoided had she not be so unreasonable.

"Well, what do you want me to say? If I come by the house and speak to him, I'm going back to jail. If I call my own house that's harassment. Nicole, why don't you tell me exactly how to handle this situation since you wanna wear the pants."

"Lance, listen, I know I might have went overboard—"

"You might have?" I sarcastically said as I cut Nicole off.

"Yeah, just hear me out. I been really praying and fasting about us and our marriage, and just about everything in general and now with this incident with LL, I know that God is trying to show me something."

I kept quiet because I knew that once Nicole got on her *God told me this, God told me that* soapbox, there was no use in trying to get in a word edgewise because it would simply go on deaf ears, so I kept my mouth shut until she was finished.

"And so your point is?" I asked sarcastically when she was done.

Nicole sucked her teeth and said, "Lance, my point is that I realize where I was wrong, but you know, you could show a little humility yourself and admit where you were wrong too."

"Nicole, show me my error? You falsely accuse me of cheating—with no evidence, I might add—

you throw me out of my own house, and get me locked up for it, and you want me to show you where I was wrong?"

There was silence on the phone, and then Nicole asked me if I would come by the house later that evening so that we could both talk with LL.

"Let me call my lawyer first and see if it's all right for me to do that. No, matter of fact, why don't you type up a letter authorizing me to come to my own house and sign it, then scan it and e-mail it to my phone. When I get that, then I'll come through."

"Lance, come on now."

"What do you mean, *Lance, come on now*? Hello! I was just locked up for five days and I'm not trying to go back to jail, so if you want me to come through then sign off on that and e-mail it to me! You created this nonsense, not me!"

"Okay, Lance, fine, I'll e-mail you a signed letter okaying you to come by the house."

I remained quiet because I was still heated, and all of the feelings that I had been feeling when I was sitting in jail were all starting to creep back up and make me even madder. I mean, it was absolutely ridiculous that I had even been locked up and put through the system. And although I didn't have a short fuse, having had my freedom taken away from me was something that didn't sit well with me and it never would, especially when it was over some bullshit.

"Well, listen, why you waited until eight-thirty at night to call me and tell me this, that I don't know . . ."

"Lance, you know I go to church on Tuesday nights; I just got out and I'm on my way back to the house."

"Well, like I was getting ready to say, T.L. is having an album release party tonight at Guesthouse in the city and I'm getting ready to head to that, so being that it's already late, why don't I just come by in the morning before you leave for work and we can talk with him then." I would always drop anything at any moment for my son, but I had a feeling that I would have to deal with some added bullshit from Nicole and so once again I had to make a shit-or-get-off-of-the-pot decision, and at that moment, I decided to shit on my situation once again.

"Who are you going to the city with?"

"With Steve."

"Lance, I'm not trying to preach to you, but don't you think you've been partying just a little bit too much lately?"

"No," I simply responded.

"Well, I don't know. Just be careful. I'll call you in the morning."

"Okay, and listen. This is just a phase for right now that will pass real soon. I told you, I'm just trying to have my face constantly in the mix until I manage to break through with this movie thing. And it's all about who you know, so if I'm not in the mix I won't be able to network and meet people."

"Yeah, Lance, I know all of that, but you're also a married man with a son. So just watch the example you set for him. And I always tell you, you don't have to chase what you can attract. When God is ready to open that movie door for you it will open, you don't have to sell your soul in the process."

I knew it was time to hang up the phone because Nicole always took it to the extreme with the religious shit. How was going to a party all of a sudden selling my soul?

"Okay, Nicole, just call me in the morning," I said to her cordially before hanging up.

There was no way in the world that I was gonna miss or even be very late for T.L.'s party. It was parties like his that I absolutely lived for. Steve was gonna go with me to the party, but we decided that we would drive separate cars just in case either one of us hooked up with something nice at the party and wanted to leave early.

As we were getting dressed, my cell phone rang, and it was a girl who went by the name of Slim Kim. Slim Kim was the publicist for the party. She had called me because I had called her earlier that day to put Mashonda and Layla on the list for the party.

"What's good, Lance? Sorry it took me so long to hit you back but today my phone is straight bananas."

"Yeah, I could imagine. I hope I'm not killing you, but I need to add four more people to the list."

"No, no, It's all good. So I already got you plus one. You want me to change that to plus five."

"Exactly."

"I gotchu, baby boy. Just get me at the bar tonight and it's all good," she said in a joking manner.

"No doubt! I gotchu, girl," I said before hanging up the phone.

Steve thought I was the biggest, lamest asshole in the world for inviting both Mashonda and Layla to the party when there was already gonna be so much brand new pussy at the party to choose from. For the most part, I understood where he was coming from and he was right, but it was my ego more than anything else that had caused me to invite them. It was like more than anything I just wanted to show them that I had the power to get them into such a high-profile party. But I was certain to tell them that I was gonna be moving around the entire night and that I wouldn't be able to really chill with them that much. So I felt like in a sense that I had covered myself by building an out for myself before the party even started.

Just before midnight me and Steve arrived at the party. The line to get inside was thick and it stretched about half a block long. But we bypassed the line and headed straight to the front. As we approached the bouncers one of them asked, "Lance, he's witchu?"

"Yeah, he's with me," I said as I waited for him to pull back the ropes so that we could enter the party, "and listen, I got about four more shorties coming through, make sure they get in, a'ight?" I said to the bouncer as I placed a hundred-dollar bill in the palm of his hand.

"That's what's up. I'm on that for you."

I knew for a fact that it was because my face had been on the front page of the newspaper, and on all of the news channels, that the bouncer had so quickly recognized me, and I loved every second of feeling like a celebrity.

The party was packed. There were literally wall-to-wall people everywhere as me and Steve snaked our way to the main level of the club and over to the bar. I saw a lot of people that I knew but I wasn't able to get everyone's attention.

"It's rammed up in here," Steve said, just before getting one of the bartender's attention and ordering drinks for the both of us.

Just as I finished my first drink, I felt my phone vibrating. I looked at it and I saw a text from Nicole that said;

> Lance, I just wanted to tell you that in spite of everything that's happened over the past week, I still love you!

I blew some air out of my lungs and I couldn't help but smile. Nicole was a special person and I knew why I loved her so much. I was happy to see her text, but again, I had to compartmentalize and move those thoughts to the back of my mind because I didn't want to feel any guilt feelings. I quickly texted back that I loved her as well, and then I put my phone away and tried to get the bartender's attention so that I could order another round of drinks. There was a young lady who was also trying to get the bartender's attention as well.

"What are you drinking? I got it!" I yelled over the music into the girl's ear.

She looked at me and smiled and then told me that it was okay, that I didn't have to do that.

"It's all good, I gotchu," I said as I finally got the bartender's attention and ordered my drink and told him to get the young lady whatever she wanted.

She smiled again and then told the bartender to let her have an apple martini.

"Thank you," she said into my ear.

I really was just being nice and wasn't even trying to kick it to her, and I could tell that she appreciated that fact. She also seemed a little bit surprised that I didn't at least ask her what her name was.

The night was real young and I was just getting warmed up so that move that I had made in buying her a drink and not asking her what her name was, it was just a move to get my swagger in full tilt.

I paid for the drinks and told the young lady to be safe and that I would see her around. Me and Steve continued making our way through the crowd and bumped into someone that we knew from Queens but we hadn't seen in a while, a dude who went by the name of Fredro.

I had known Fredro since I was in junior high school. He was one of those pretty boy dudes from way back in the day who always had money, the baddest chicks and the baddest cars. When all of the money from the crack game started to dry up, Fredro was one of the first dudes from New York to go down to Virginia to get money dealing weight. So he was well-known for his flamboyance and for always holding money.

"Oh shit, my niggas! What up?" Fredro said as he gave us a pound.

"What's the deal?" Steve replied.

Fredro told us to follow him and that he and his crew had a table upstairs near the other bar.

"Yo, we got the whole upstairs on smash, come on."

As we followed Fredro I was directly behind him and while we were on the winding steps that lead to upstairs, Fredro turned to me and in my ear and said, "Yo, I got that *white*. Holla at your boy!"

I nodded and the three of us kept it moving. When we finally did make it upstairs, the energy was totally different than it had been downstairs. Downstairs was much more rammed and people were more or less profiling, but upstairs people were actually partying their asses off and having a good time.

I immediately recognized Buffie the Body, DJ Kay Slay was in the spot chillin'. Toccara from *America's Next Top Model* was there, Roxie from BET's *106 & Park* was there. I saw one of the NY Jets, and I also saw the model Melyssa Ford. Steve saw something that he liked and he told me that he was gonna be back so that he could go holla at the chick.

After Steve walked off, I went up to Fredro and I handed him two hundred dollars. He looked down at the money and without saying anything he went into his pocket and discreetly pulled out two cellophane bags of cocaine and handed them to me.

"The bouncer at the bathroom all the way in the back, he knows what up." Fredro said right before breaking out into a quick, impromptu P. Diddy dance move that was right on cue with the DJ throwing on "Hypnotized" by the Notorious B.I.G.

"No doubt," I said as I calmly walked off to the bathroom.

I hadn't done coke in a while, but I was skilled at it and I didn't need the bouncer to keep people out of the bathroom for me since I didn't stretch out my coke and snort lines of it at a time. All I needed was the car key from my key chain and I was good to go. I missed doing coke and with all of this stress that was going on with Nicole it was like the perfect excuse for me to try some.

I went into one of the bathroom stalls and carefully opened up one of the bags of cocaine and stuck my key into it until there was a small mountain of cocaine sitting on my key. I slowly lifted the key to my right nostril while I used the index finger from my left hand and pinched my left nostril, and then with my right nostril I snorted the coke. I did that about ten times and then I put the cocaine away, put the keys in my pocket and I wiped my nose and exited the bathroom.

By the time I made it back over to Fredro and his crew, I was high as a fucking kite. The cocaine mixed with the alcohol was the ultimate high.

"You shining!" Fredro said as he gave me a pound. "It's off the hook, right?"

I was almost too high to speak, so all I did was smile at Fredro and nod my head. With the cocaine running through my system I had all of the confidence in the world and began dancing with different chicks and trying to rap to just about any and every chick, but I was in control of myself and I made sure I did things in a tasteful way.

Steve didn't fuck with any type of drugs. No X-pills, no coke, and no weed. All he did was drink and I respected that since he was fearful of violating his job's drug policy and potentially losing his well-paying city job.

I was so high that I didn't even care that both Layla and Mashonda were looking for me. Normally I would have been a little bit stressed-out and panicked since they had both texted me within five minutes apart and told me that they had arrived and asked me where I was. I texted them both back and told them where I was, but before they reached me I had went back into the bathroom to snort some more coke.

When I came out, I saw Slim Kim.

"What's up, Mama?" I gave her a hug and a kiss on the cheek and she asked me if I was having a good time.

When I was done speaking with her, Mashonda walked up to me from behind and she wrapped her arms around my waist.

"Hey sexy!" I said as I kissed her on her lips.

Mashonda then introduced me to the two people she was with. Both of them were just as sexy as she was and they both had bodies like she did. One of the chicks was named Felicia, who was her older cousin from New York, And the other chick that she introduced me to was named Joy, who she introduced as her mother.

"Get the fuck outta here!" I said over the loud music. "There's no way that's your mother."

All three of them laughed because they said they always got the same reaction from people. I called Steve over and introduced him to Mashonda and her family and he too couldn't believe that Mashonda was standing there with her mother.

Mashonda, Felicia, and Joy were all dressed in real expensive high-end designer shit. Mashonda was wearing Diane von Furstenberg, Felicia was wearing Tory Burch, and Joy was wearing Zac Posen.

"So do I call you Mrs. Williams or Joy?" I asked as I looked at her left hand and noticed that she was wearing a wedding ring.

"I would be offended if you didn't call me Joy," she replied.

At that moment, Layla walked up to me wearing some tight jeans and high heels and this see-through chiffon turtleneck sweater. It was clearly obvious that she had no bra underneath because you could see her titties right through the top, areola and all. Layla kissed me on the cheek and she said hello to Steve but she stood right by my side. I played things cool and introduced her to everybody. It was a real awkward feeling because I could sense that some ghettoness was getting ready to come from Mashonda and her cousin Felicia.

Thankfully, Steve stepped up and said that he was buying drinks and asked everybody what they were drinking. That gave me time to walk off with Layla.

"You are murdering that top."

"Who were them chicks? One of them wasn't your wife, was it?"

"Nah, my wife isn't here, they just some people that I know, they cool, though."

"Oh, 'cause I'm just saying, one of them was looking at me with this stank look, and—"

"Layla, just chill. They cool. We gonna all chill tonight and have a good time, a'ight?"

"Yeah, I'm good but I will check a bitch up in here, that's all I'm saying."

I blew some air from my lungs and walked off by myself and headed back to the bathroom to snort some more coke. I told Layla to chill with Steve until I got back.

I made it to the bathroom and I stayed there for about five minutes snorting my ass off until I had completely finished one of the hundred-dollar bags of coke that I had.

When I exited the bathroom, the bouncer asked me if I was a'ight. I knew that he knew what I was doing and so I wondered if I was giving off a stoned high look or something.

"Yeah, I'm cool," I said. And just as I finished saying that I quickly glanced to my right as someone walked by me.

"Toni?" I said, unsure if that was her.

The young lady stopped in her tracks and turned around, and it was indeed Toni.

I don't know what it was about Toni, but literally every time I saw her she would cause me to feel these uncontrollable feelings that reminded me of a teenage crush or something. It was like a mixture of excitement, lust, and love all wrapped up in one.

Toni was wearing a nice Gucci dress that showed off her body in a very tasteful way. I wanted to give her a hug but for some reason I felt awkward and I didn't want to come across like she had this power over me.

"Hey!" she said.

"I didn't know you were here."

"Well, I knew you were in here," she replied kind of snappy.

"What the hell does that mean?" I asked.

"It doesn't mean anything, but Lance, you *really* should just get a drink in your hand and go and chill. You'all running around, talking to every woman in here, like you some undersexed teenager or something. That is so tired and tacky. You look very thirsty!"

"Why are you coming for my neck? And what the hell are you so concerned with what I'm doing?" Toni knew just the right buttons to push to chump me and make me feel like an asshole. Despite being high as a kite, her words still managed to cut me.

Toni shook her head as if she was disgusted but she didn't say anything.

"And you know that shit was fucked up that you couldn't even call me to check on a nigga these past few days and I know you saw on the news what I was going through."

"Lance, I did call you. Three times, as a matter of fact, but your voice mail was full, so what was I supposed to do?"

"Then you shoulda texted me."

"Oh, please."

"So I know you here with your record-mogul husband," I said.

"Yes, I am here with Keith. And your point in saying that was? I mean, why wouldn't I be here with him?"

"Where you should be is home with my daughter! You saying I'm running around looking tired, well, it's just as tired for you to be a thirty-one-year-old woman out partying on a Tuesday night when your daughter got school the next morning. Toni, you ain't twenty-five years old anymore, take your ass home to your daughter!"

"Lance, you know what? I know you're high right now, so I won't even respond to that nonsense. And seriously, if you're gonna do coke, at least wipe the cocaine from your nose! Jesus Christ!" she said and shook her head.

I felt stupid as I quickly ran my hand across my face to wipe the cocaine residue from my nose.

"Thank you!" she added.

I laughed and replied, "Damn, you really must not be getting fucked right 'cause your ass is so uptight."

"Lance, first of all, let me tell you something. I ain't one of these little hood-rat chicks that you up in here hollering at, okay? So if you gonna talk to me you talk to me with some respect or don't say shit to me at all! And for the record, Keith is the *only* one that is fucking me and knows *how* to fuck me. Okay? Unlike you and your pencil dick, when Keith fucks me I actually have an orgasm so let's be clear! And since you on this disrespectful shit, now is as good a time as any to let you know that I'm filing the papers to change Sahara's last name to Keith's last name. You may be Sahara's father but Keith is her daddy!"

I clenched my teeth because I almost lost my temper, and it took everything in me not to slap fire out of Toni's ass at that moment. I knew that I was getting ready to go back to jail for assault because Toni had purposely tried to get under my skin, and she definitely succeeded.

But thank God, right at that moment Mashonda, who was going to the bathroom, walked up to me.

"Oh, there you go, baby. You okay?"

"Yeah, I'm cool," I said as Toni shook her head and walked off, continuing on to the bathroom.

"That liquor is ready to come out, where is the bathroom?" Mashonda asked.

I knew that I didn't want Mashonda in the bathroom at the same time with Toni so I asked her to just chill with me for a minute.

"No, Lance, you don't understand, if I don't get to a bathroom and pee like right now, it's gonna be a problem."

I walked up to the bouncer and I gave him a hundred dollars and I asked him if he could let me have the bathroom to myself for a while.

"Fifteen minutes, a'ight?" he responded while barely flinching.

I nodded my head and then I grabbed Mashonda by the hand and told her to come with me to the guy's bathroom. She followed behind me and without hesitation she went directly into one of the stalls and did her thing.

When Mashonda was finished peeing she began washing her hands and that's when I took out the bag of coke that I had and held it in my left hand and plucked it two times with the middle finger of my right hand in order to cause the cocaine to sift to the bottom.

"You ever do this?" I asked Mashonda.

She shook her head *no* and by the look on her face I could tell that she wasn't all that keen on messing with it.

"This is the best drug in the world. It's better than weed because the high is better and you don't have to worry about your hands and your clothes smelling like weed," I said as I dipped my car key into the bag and put a small pile of cocaine on it and brought it to my nose and snorted just as I had been doing all night long.

"And it's better than liquor because you don't smell like liquor and you don't have to worry about no hangovers like you do with alcohol."

Mashonda just looked at me as I dipped into the bag again and snorted some more coke. I wondered what was going through her mind and what she was thinking about me at that moment.

"Does it sting when you snort it?" she asked.

"Nah, not to me it doesn't. I don't even feel it."

With Mashonda's question I knew that she would be down to experiment with me so without asking her I carefully put some more coke on the tip of the key and I brought it toward Mashonda's face and instructed her on how to snort it. She did as I told her, and after blinking her eyes a few times she smiled.

"You gotta give it a minute or so to take effect," I explained as I raised some more coke to her face and she snorted that too.

After about three minutes Mashonda told me that she was feeling nice and she asked me if she could get some more.

"Nah, that's all you get, baby, just have a drink when we go back out and you'll be straight."

She smiled and told me that she was already straight. Then she walked up to me and kissed me and told me that she had missed me.

"I missed you too," I said as I kissed her back.

After a minute or so of heavy kissing and feeling on each other, me and Mashonda both had our pants down to our ankles and I was fucking her doggystyle as she braced herself by placing both of her hands on the sink.

I was high as a kite and that was what clouded my judgment and caused me to run up in Mashonda raw. Her pussy felt so much better this time than it had when I had fucked her in the hotel room, and I knew that was because the cocaine running through my body was enhancing everything, and also because sex always felt better without a condom.

Mashonda tried her hardest to not make noise. I could tell that she wanted to completely let loose. I knew that I had to hurry up because the bouncer was only gonna let us stay in there for so long. But within like five minutes I was cumming and I didn't even bother to pull out.

"You came inside of me?" Mashonda asked somewhat nervously.

"That shit felt too good to pull out!" I explained.

"You know I should bust you in your head, right?" Mashonda said as she playfully punched me on my shoulder before asking me get her a paper towel. She wiped herself and then pulled her pants back up and the two of us prepared to walk back out into the party.

"My pussy gonna be leaking all night because of you, but that was fun!" Mashonda devilishly said.

At that point, as we went back among the people, I felt like an absolute king, like I was on top of the world. I was wilding out and living crazy out of control and I knew that I would have to reign myself in, but there was no way I was gonna slow down for the rest of that night.

From that twenty minutes or so that I had been away from the bathroom, the party got even more packed than it had been. I couldn't locate Steve, and I didn't see Layla, so I figured that they were probably together. Mashonda walked off and told me that she was gonna go try and find her cousin and her mom.

I made my way over to the VIP area and Slim Kim introduced me to T.L. and asked me to pose with him for a picture, which I had no problem doing.

"Hey you," someone said to me and pinched my stomach.

I turned and saw that it was Meagan from *Media Edition*. Meagan was drop-dead gorgeous and she was the type of woman who I would definitely want to marry in my next lifetime. I was happy to see her but I was hoping that she didn't know I was high.

"How you doing, Ms. Washington?"

"I'm chillin'. I didn't know you were gonna be here, you ok?" she shouted in my ear.

"Yeah, I'm good. It's good seeing you again."

"You too! And listen, I didn't forget to call you, I just got tied up earlier in the day today."

"It's all good. Don't worry, I'm here. Just hit me up when you can."

Meagan nodded and then grabbed my hand and pulled me toward her so that I could dance with her.

As soon as we started dancing, I looked to my left and I saw Toni and her husband Keith. Toni looked at me and shook her head. I just ignored her and kept dancing with Meagan.

"You look nice," I said in Meagan's ear while we danced.

Meagan thanked me for the compliment. I was still high as a kite and so I had to make sure that I maintained in front of Meagan and didn't come across in a way that would turn her off and cause her to never follow up with me for that interview.

"Can I just be honest with you about something?" I asked.

"Of course."

"I have to tell you that I've always had the biggest crush on you. You always reminded me of Nia Long whenever I saw you on TV."

Meagan smiled and she replied, "Oh, so you really mean that you always had a crush on Nia Long."

She had the perfect comeback, and I really didn't know what to say, so I just smiled and told her that I liked her style.

"So whether we do the interview or not, would you ever let me take you out to dinner, or breakfast?"

"Like on a date, you mean?" Meagan asked with a smile. "Lance, aren't you married?"

I didn't respond.

She shook her head, then said, "Don't do it to yourself, Lance."

"Don't do it to myself?" I asked.

"Yeah, that's what I said."

"Why you say that?" I asked Meagan as we stopped dancing and I walked over with her to sit down.

"I'll be straight up with you just like I am with everybody else. You wouldn't be able to afford me and honestly, you can't handle this. I'm not trying to be conceited or whatever, but I'm just straight up."

"Wow. A'ight, a'ight. I respect that. Like I said, I like your style."

"You like my style? So what's your style, tell me where you live?"

"I live in Great Neck, Long Island."

Meagan nodded and smiled.

"Okay, tell me about your cars," Meagan asked.

"I push three two cars and a truck. I got the 2009 Range Rover. I got the 2008 650i convertible BMW and I got the CLS Benz coupe."

Meagan looked at me and nodded her head and she said that she was impressed.

"So, did I pass your test?"

"You passed the entrance exam to take me out to dinner, but this right here, this is passport pussy. I'm just being straight up," Meagan said with a look of all seriousness.

"You was drinking tonight, wasn't you?"

Meagan laughed and then she punched me on my arm and told me that she was just joking with me. But in my heart of hearts I knew that she was straight up and with her it was about the dollars, and I had dollars, so I knew that I was gonna get with that.

"I'm gonna go mingle but I'll definitely call you so we can do that interview for the show."

"Let me get your number," I said to her as I pulled out my phone. She had tried to give me the number the day before so I knew that it would be no problem in getting it from her.

"So you working with passport pussy? I like that. I'm gonna put a bunch a stamps in that passport," I said to her before she walked off.

Meagan didn't respond but she did smile as she walked off.

I had completely lost track of time as the night wore on. I had lost Mashonda and her crew, but it was cool since I had already hit it, I didn't really want to see her again. I had managed to catch up with Layla and she basically hawked me for the rest of the night, but it was all good because I chilled at the bar downstairs with her and drank shots of Patrón until we were both ready to leave.

Layla had taken the train to the city so she asked me to drive her back home to Brooklyn, which I agreed to do. So around three-thirty in the morning we left the club together and headed to my BMW, which was parked about three blocks away.

I knew that Layla was probably in the mood to fuck, but I was so fucked-up from the cocaine and all the liquor that I had consumed that all I wanted to do was jump in the shower real quick and get my ass in a bed and recover. Plus, it was cold and it was just starting to snow, so all of those factors combined just sealed my decision that I wasn't gonna make pussy a priority.

We made it to the Brooklyn Bridge and it was weird because a big part of me didn't even really remember what streets I had taken to get to the bridge. All I knew was that one minute we were leaving the club and the next minute I was crossing the bridge. And just as I thought, Layla was feeling frisky and she reached over and began unbuckling my pants and started stroking my dick.

As soon as my dick was hard, she unbuckled her seat belt and placed her head in my lap and started sucking my dick. The music was blasting and the streets were empty so I was breezing through the streets and catching all of the green lights.

Even though I didn't feel like fucking, getting a blow job was the perfect nightcap. Whenever I drank it always took me longer to cum, and that night was no exception, and Layla was really working hard to get me to cum. And five minutes into the blow job I could tell that I was gonna buss real soon, but unfortunately the next thing I remember is hearing the sound of screeching tires. I looked up and the last thing I remember was seeing bright lights practically blinding me.

"Oh, shit!" I screamed.

Boom!

That was the sound I heard, followed by shattering glass that hit me in the face. Both the driver's side and the passenger side air bags released. I remember feeling like the wind had been knocked out of me and a sharp pain was shooting up my leg. My car came to a dead stop and I remember hearing a hissing sound and the sound of a horn that wouldn't shut off. I had no idea what I had hit but I knew that I had hit something.

"Layla, you all right?" I asked, although I could barely talk since I couldn't breathe.

Layla responded that she was a little banged up but that she thought she was okay.

I remember thinking to myself that I had to hurry up and exit the car because for some reason I just felt like we were gonna be hit by another car. So immediately I tried to open my door but the door wasn't budging. Then I looked to my right and I realized that the entire passenger side had been pushed in crazy. And what was wild is that the way it was pushed in I realized that if Layla hadn't been giving me a blow job that she would have definitely been killed, because it was like that whole side of the car had been pushed in and was collapsed around us.

My heart started racing from fear and I realized that we were both trapped in the car. All of a sudden I got really dizzy and everything started spinning around, and I felt real light-headed. I remember hearing this ringing sound in my ears and the sound became deafening. I remember thinking about my son LL, and about my daughter Sahara. Then I remembered an image of my mother's face flash in front of my eyes. And before I knew it, I had passed out and my body was slumped in my seat and on top of Layla's.

When I came to, I remember seeing lights and people everywhere. I also remember shivering uncontrollably, but although my body was shivering I was immobilized on a stretcher, I couldn't move my limbs and my neck was in some sort of plastic brace.

"What happened?" I remember sounding those words to one of the firemen that was standing near my stretcher. My words were barely audible but he did hear me. And then he told me to relax and that I had been involved in a serious car accident.

"Can you tell me your name?" one of the paramedics asked me. "How old are you? What year is it? Do you know who the president is?"

The paramedic was asking me those questions in an attempt to gauge how badly I was hurt.

I didn't answer his questions, partly because I wasn't sure of the answers but mainly because I was cold as hell and I couldn't breathe.

"I can't breathe," I mumbled.

He told me to relax and that they were gonna get me some oxygen as soon as they loaded me into the ambulance. Within seconds I remember being hoisted into the ambulance and seeing the doors close and speeding off with the sound of a siren glaring in the background.

I definitely felt like I was dreaming and at the same time I didn't know if I was dead. But I do know that I was in tremendous pain, and so I just closed my eyes and began praying to God.

Chapter Ten

When I woke up, the first person that I saw standing next to me was Nicole.

"Baby, what happened? Where am I?"

Nicole explained that I had been in a terrible car accident and that I was in Brookdale Hospital in Brooklyn. I could tell that she had been crying at some point, but I could also see a look of sternness mixed into her face.

Before Nicole and I could really begin talking, a detective stepped up to the other side of my bed and introduced himself and showed me his badge while his partner stood at the foot of my bed.

"Mr. Thomas, I'm Detective Gasparino from Brooklyn North, and this is Detective Joseph."

After getting the introductions out of the way, Detective Gasparino told me that he was placing me under arrest.

"Under arrest for what?"

"For the possession of a controlled substance," he coldly said and proceeded to read me my rights.

I frowned and looked at Nicole, and she exhaled and shook her head. When the detective was done he placed one handcuff on my wrist and he placed the other handcuff on the rail of the bed.

"What the fuck is going on?"

"Lance, the paramedics found a small amount of cocaine in your pants pocket when they were looking for your identification."

I exhaled and swallowed very hard. I knew I was fucked and I didn't know what else to say.

The detective then informed me that they wanted to draw blood to test the blood-alcohol content but they had to read me something called my chemical rights. They explained that I had the right to refuse to have my blood drawn, but if I refused my license would immediately be suspended and that I would be hit with an additional criminal charge for refusing.

"I'm not submitting to no test. Nah, I'm sorry, you can't draw my blood for that."

The detective looked at Nicole, and apparently she had already informed them that she was an attorney and that she was also my wife.

"Lance, listen, just let them draw the blood and take the test. They already found cocaine on you so if you refuse they'll be back in an hour with a search warrant from a judge giving them permission to take your blood without your consent."

I shook my head and told them to just do whatever they had to do. So they called for a nurse and she proceeded to draw blood from my arm. The detective exchanged cards with Nicole and they soon left but a uniformed police officer stood guard right outside my room.

"Lance, what in Jesus' name were you thinking?" Nicole asked me. I could tell that she was disgusted.

I rolled my eyes and blew more air out of my lungs. The sheer terror and fear that I was feeling at that moment was beyond human words. I mean, in like a split second I went from partying with stars and being on top of the world to facing some serious life-altering shit. Shit that I wasn't prepared for, nor did I know how to prepare myself for what was to come.

"I hope you know you just ruined your life! You do know that?"

"Why you gotta always be so dramatic? I made a mistake. It happened, what can I do?" I said, trying not to show my true feelings of fear.

"A mistake, Lance? Lance, a car accident—yes, that is a mistake. But driving drunk and high on cocaine—that isn't a mistake! Driving in the wrong direction on Flatbush Avenue—Lance, that isn't a mistake! What were you thinking?"

Oh, shit! I thought to myself.

I had no idea that I had been driving on the wrong side of the street. But apparently after I'd come off of the Brooklyn Bridge and I turned on to Flatbush Avenue, I turned into the northbound lanes when I should have turned into the southbound lanes and I collided with a small Toyota Corolla right in front of the famous Junior's restaurant.

Nicole started crying as she told me that I had killed a twenty-four-year-old woman and badly injured her fiancé.

"What?" I asked in disbelief.

"Yes, Lance. Oh my God, I can't believe this is happening," she stated while burying her head into her hands.

There are absolutely no words in the human language that can describe how bad I was feeling at that moment. I was feeling a sense of desperation and helplessness but I had no words simply because there were no words that could explain or make up for what I had done. The bottom line was that I was scared as hell, and at the same time I was feeling a ton of regret. Like I just kept thinking over and over that at the end of the day I was in this position simply because of pussy, and wasn't no extramarital pussy worth what I was going through.

"And Lance, who is the lady that was in your car with you?" Nicole asked. She was visibly holding back tears.

"She was just a friend. One of Steve's friends."

Nicole came close to my bed and she placed her hands on the rails and tears began to stream down her face.

She leaned in a little bit and with controlled anger said, "The day you told me that Toni was pregnant by you I thought that was the worst day in my life and it was something that I would wish on no woman. But when the police call my house before the crack of dawn and tell me that my husband was involved in a car accident and that I needed to get to the hospital, I immediately start thinking the worst. And that feeling that came over me, thinking that you might have been killed—I can tell you that felt worst than knowing what you had done with Toni. And then I get here and there are cops everywhere, so I identify myself first as your lawyer and not your wife, because with the number of cops that were here, and with the media, I knew something wasn't right. And then they tell me that they suspected you were drinking. And in my head I say, okay, it's stupid, but what can you do? Then they tell me about the cocaine and they tell me there was another woman in your car and that the firemen and paramedics initially found you with your pants unbuckled and your penis exposed! I said to myself that someone had to be playing a dirty trick on me, because there is no way that you could be that stupid! There's just no way! And then they tell me about the fatality and I knew that this whole episode had topped Toni's pregnancy."

"Baby, just hear me—"

"No! I am not hearing you out! I am so sick and tired of being sick and tired!"

"Baby, don't walk out on me like this, not now!" I pleaded because I could tell that Nicole was ready to leave the hospital.

"First of all, I am not your baby. Let's get that straight. And second . . ." Nicole paused for a moment and pinched the bridge of her nose and shook her head before continuing on. "You know what? Forget it. It's not even worth the stress. I'm gonna call Attorney Jones and I'll have him represent you because I just can't do this anymore. I can't, Lance. I just can't. I mean, you have *no idea*, no idea at all how much I love you."

"Baby, yes I do."

"No, you don't, because if you did, you wouldn't put me through this. And God only knows what else you've done and what you're capable of still doing. I mean, I thought I had over-reacted by putting you out the house and I wanted to reverse that and have us move on, and then this." Nicole shook her head and began crying much harder.

"Here, take this," she said as she took off her wedding ring and placed it in the palm of my hand and folded my fingers over it.

"What are you doing?"

"I'm leaving you."

"Nicole!" I shouted as she turned and started to walk out of the room.

She turned back toward me and then she said, "In your heart of hearts, you know you had already walked out on me a long time ago."

"I never left you and I would never leave you, you know that," I desperately said.

"Lance, listen to me. I said, in your heart you've already left me and you can look at your left hand and it will tell you the exact same thing that I'm saying."

"What are you talking about?"

"I gave you my wedding ring, Lance. And I had it on my finger to give to you. Even in our roughest times I never went without wearing my ring because I knew what it represented. But you, I don't even have to ask you why you aren't wearing your ring because I know why it's not on your finger I know why and you know why."

Nicole took one more long look at me, and then she turned and walked out of the room for good.

I was speechless because to me it was like, what do I say? Nicole had pulled my card. She was right about everything she said. The sad part was that I had made it a lame habit of taking off my wedding ring in certain circumstances. I did it deliberately and it was stupid but at the same time in my heart I knew that I loved Nicole. It was just that I was constantly feeling conflicted. Conflicted about doing the right thing versus doing the selfish thing. I hated feeling that way, and in all honesty I hated cheating, and yet cheating made me feel normal on some level. It was like cheating calmed me and made me feel whole. So in some sense I was like the person who loved to drink and had a ball getting drunk, but yet I hated the hangovers and the consequences of drinking. But just like it's not until a drunk is hungover and worshiping the toilet bowl, while puking his guts out, does he realize how good it feels to be sober And with the asshole that I was, it took dire consequences like I was going through for me to realize just how much I loved and valued the calm, relaxed, monogamous family life.

What's wild is that on a subconscious level I know I was living crazy and disrespecting Nicole because I knew that I could get away with it. Like I never, ever believed that she had it in her to put her foot down and say enough is enough. And just like a child will test a parent and push the limits of what they can get away with, and keep pushing those limits until the parent smacks the shit out of them and forces the child to show some goddamn respect for the parent-child relationship, I knew how to push the limits of my marriage because I never feared Nicole's reaction. But this time it was different. I could feel it and I knew that Nicole was done, that she had had enough of my shit and it made me feel numb to even think about life without my wife. I was determined to set things straight again and get everything back on the right course.

I had fucked up big-time, but I was only at the tip of the iceberg in terms of really realizing how many lives I had royally screwed up.

Chapter Eleven

I forget exactly what time it was that Nicole had left the hospital. The sun was up. And since it was the dead of winter, the sun didn't come up until about 7:00 A.M. or so. So I knew that it had to be after 7:00 A.M. But with the way things had been moving so fast it was probably more like twelve-thirty in the afternoon. But even though it was a bitterly cold winter day, the New York media proved that they would stop at nothing to get at the heart of a breaking story such as mine.

The media had gotten wind of the car accident when it was transmitted over the police scanners and all of the major newspapers and news stations dispatched crews to the scene of the accident and to the hospital. My accident was the lead story on the six A.M. newscasts.

In fact, it wasn't until I had my nurse turn on the television in my room that I was able to realize the extent of the damages to both my car and to the car that I had hit. Both cars were almost unrecognizable. It was also from the news that I learned that Layla and I had to be cut out of the car. And of course, when the media found out that I was the one who was driving the car and that I was suspected of driving while under the influence, they went crazy with the story.

I was watching the local ABC news channel and I couldn't believe how fast that they had gotten all of the details. They knew that I had been coming from an album release party for T.L. and they knew that I had just been placed under arrest for being in possession of a controlled substance. Other than the devastation that I had caused the innocent victims, the thing that I focused on the most was when the reporters spoke about all of the possible criminal charges that I was facing.

I had written about gangsta shit in my novels and about killings and drugs and jail and all of that. But this was no book that I was writing. This was real life. It was my life. And never in my wildest dreams did I see myself as the going-to-prison type. I wasn't built for prison. So, although I was feeling horrible and scared as all hell, I knew that I had to scan my brain and get in touch with as many people as I could who could help me and go to bat for me. My ass was in a serious sling and my neck was in a noose that was getting tighter by the second.

At the same time as I watched the news coverage and feared and worried about what was to come, I couldn't help but feel extremely remorseful for the damage I had caused to the victims of the other families. And regardless of what would happen to me and what jail time I was going to face, I was determined to not let this be one of those times where I painted myself as the victim in order to deflect attention from the real victims in this tragedy, because it was clear who those victims were. Just as it was clear who was the major asshole in this whole ordeal—that being, my black ass.

Eventually, the doctor came to my room and explained to me that I had a severely sprained ankle and my right lung had also collapsed and that I would need to have quick, minor surgery to reinflate my lung.

"Surgery?"

"Yes, it's nothing major. We'll give you a local anesthetic and then make a small incision in between your ribs. Once we do that we will insert a tube that will allow for the reinflation of the lung."

By 4:00 P.M. that same day, I was able to leave the hospital. I was accompanied by Attorney

Jones, my mother, and Steve. Unfortunately for me I wasn't able to just hop in a car and go home. I was handcuffed and flanked on both sides of me by New York City police officers who were escorting me to a Brooklyn police precinct for processing, and then I would be heading off to jail before seeing a judge.

It's funny, because although no one wants to go to jail, I knew that jail was what I deserved. I knew that, simply because it was very unfair that I was able to just walk out of the hospital with all of my physical faculties functioning okay, all the while I had put someone's lifeless body in a morgue and I had another victim fighting for his life with severe injuries. I desperately wanted to go and apologize to my victims and their families, but on the advice of my lawyer, I decided against it for the time being.

Anyway, I ended up spending the night in jail, and the next day I went before a judge inside of a jam-packed downtown Brooklyn courtroom. The judge read me the riot act and he rightly so ripped into my ass in a stern, but eloquent, way as I stood before him as humbly as I possibly could.

The judge was careful not to talk to me as if I had been tried and convicted of my crime. But reading between the lines he knew that I was guilty. Since this was just my arraignment, he could only say but so much.

It wasn't like I was going to jail right there at that moment so I wasn't too nervous. But just the mere fact of me standing in front of a judge was sort of surreal. It was almost like an out-of-body experience. I had this feeling of embarrassment mixed with disbelief as I listened to the judge.

I had been charged with aggravated vehicular manslaughter, a crime that, in New York, carries a maximum of twenty-five years in prison. I had also been charged with driving under the influence, the possession of a controlled substance, and I was hit with various traffic infractions.

But since the cocaine amount that I had on me at the time of the accident was such a small amount, the most serious charge by far that I was facing was the aggravated vehicular manslaughter charge.

Attorney Jones was no slouch. He was one of the most prominent black attorneys in the New York City metropolitan area. So in a respectful way, he made sure that he checked the judge on how he was talking to me, all the while my lawyer made sure that he was honorable but he had to make sure that my legal interest were protected. He reminded the judge that I was in a position to make bail and that I had also been made perfectly aware that my license had been suspended, and that under no circumstances would I be operating a vehicle in the near future.

"So with all due respect, Your Honor, to both you and the families involved in this tragedy, my client is ready to post bail. All we ask is that we be given just a fair shot to present the full facts of this case before a jury and not at this arraignment."

Since I had just been arrested with the incident with Nicole, the judge had the power to deny my bail and he knew that and thankfully, by the grace of God, he had saw fit to grant me bail, but he warned me that if I were to get in trouble for anything—even if it was as small of an infraction as jaywalking—that he would have me locked up until my trial.

"Do you understand that, Mr. Thomas?"

I told the judge that I did and some more words were spoken by my lawyer, the district attorney and the judge, and before long I was allowed to leave.

When I left the courthouse the questioning that I received from the media was intense, not to mention the blistering threats and insults that were hurled at me by protesters who supported causes such as Mothers Against Drunk Drivers. I knew what kind of person I really was, but with seeing and hearing all of the protesters I have to admit that I was feeling mad, embarrassed, and ashamed; I just couldn't show it.

I left with my attorney and we went straight to his Brooklyn office.

When I got there, after limping into the elevator and making my way to the conference table he had in one of the rooms where I sat, that was when it seemed like all the pressure that had been mounting up on me hit me and came raining down like a ton of bricks. I couldn't believe that I had actually took someone's life. I mean, from day one of the accident I knew what I had done, but it was like for some reason I was just feeling all of the anxiety and pressure all at once. Like it was really real! It wasn't a game.

The person that I had killed was a Puerto Rican girl name Olivia Rodriguez. She and her fiancé worked in downtown Brooklyn at the New York City Transit Authority headquarters and they were apparently on their way to work, just three blocks away, when I hit them.

I shook my head and closed my eyes and before long tears streamed down my face because I truly, truly, truly was sorry and I did feel bad. And I was man enough to show and express my emotions.

My attorney walked into the room, along with one of his junior attorneys, and he told me that he understood the emotional turmoil that I was going through.

"I swear it was just a mistake," I said as I shook my head and buried them into my hands.

"Lance, mistakes happen and that's why we have a legal system and a legal process that allows us to put forth a defense. And we have experience in these kind of cases."

"So then—just be straight with me—that aggravated vehicular manslaughter charge comes with twenty-five years. Am I really looking at that?"

"Yes and no. Yes, that is the max that you could be hit with, but no, I doubt that you really will be hit with that. But listen, let's just back up, and I want you to tell me every detail that happened during that night that lead up to the arrest. Like where were you coming from, what did you have to drink that night, who did you come in contact with. I need you to leave out nothing. I need everyone's name that you spoke to that night. I want to know their relationship in your life. Everything. You understand?"

I nodded my head *yes*.

"Lance, for example, I know you're married to Nicole, but if the woman that was in the car with you at that time of the night wasn't Nicole, I need to know her background and the nature of your relationship with her. How did you get the cocaine, all of that. Don't leave out anything. And I also need to know the full gamut of your health history, even if it's embarrassing—just let me know. I say all of this because based on what you tell me, that is what's gonna guide us in a defense strategy. Do you understand?"

I told my lawyer that I did understand, and then I proceeded to tell him everything that I knew. As I spoke, he and the junior attorney took notes and asked me questions when they needed clarification.

We spoke at length for about an hour and when we were done I was spent. Like with everything that I didn't want to deal with, I was good at blocking things out of my mind. And I had been doing that to some extent with the accident. But being that I was forced to relive the events when discussing it with my attorney, it was like being forced to live through your worst phobia.

My attorney explained to me that I would likely avoid jail time but that I was likely going to have to pay through the nose, in terms of giving the families financial compensation.

"You know, I need to be clear. That's the scenario that I see. I mean, we will put forth an aggressive defense, but based on the facts in this case, and based on the success that you've had as a writer, the worst-case scenario is always gonna be out there. And that's that you get convicted criminally on the aggravated vehicular man-slaughter charge and you still get banged for a huge judgment in a civil case."

"So basically I could end up broke and in jail?"

"That's the worst-case. But I can tell you this, you gotta keep your nose clean. You gotta keep a low profile and you gotta hope and pray that the victims' families have a compassionate disposi-tion. I say that because we're gonna eventually try and bargain with the district attorney, but in an emotional case such as this, the district at-torney is gonna consult with the victim's families and basically let the families have the final say as to whether or not they are willing to accept any type of plea bargain."

"Wow," was all I could say as I sat there.

This entire ordeal had definitely humbled me and I knew that I had to make some serious changes and those changes were going to start that night.

That night I ended up staying at my mother's house, and I prayed and prayed and prayed like I had never in my life prayed before. And as I prayed, I knew that my success as an author had translated into financial success and that financial success had given me all kinds of freedom in terms of my time. But in the end I knew that I had misused that time. I apologized to no end to God during my prayers.

When I was done praying, I took hold of my cell phone and went into my mother's kitchen and I ran water into a big pot that she had near the sink. I dropped my BlackBerry into the pot of water and left it there for about an hour before throwing it away.

I knew that I had to make changes, and that those changes would not come unless I first cut off all of my old influences and I stopped partying like a lunatic. And that is exactly what I was determined to do.

Chapter Twelve

In my short thirty-four years, there was something that I had learned but at times I would often lose sight of it. And that was that women rarely fucked a nigga unless they had some kind of ulterior motive. Eight out of ten times the ulterior motive that women were after was money. So in other words, there was rarely a time that women would fuck for free. They rarely would straight up ask for cash in exchange for letting a dude sex them, instead what they would do is be patient and look for a payoff somewhere down the road.

Three months after I had the car accident, I was doing a very good job of staying on the straight and narrow. I was keeping my nose clean. I wasn't partying. I started going back to church on a regular basis. I wasn't in contact with people I had no business associating with. Basically, I had fallen off the radar and I had moved in with my mother. Nicole had legally separated from me and I knew that she was dead serious about going through with divorcing my no-good ass. The best thing that I had going for me was that I was spending a lot of good, quality time with my son LL and with my illegitimate daughter Sahara.

I had lost contact with Mashonda and Layla. Although I was now legally separated from Nicole and could have been spending as much time with Mashonda and Layla if I wanted to, the fact still remained that I wasn't yet divorced so I knew that I shouldn't just wild out. And in addition to that, I was really trying to do right by both God and my lawyer. So staying off the radar was the best thing for me.

During the time that I was off the radar, both Mashonda and Layla showed why they had ever really fucked with me. It was all about dollars to them, and they showed their true colors. They saw me as a cash cow. Since they never got any money out of me, they decided to take a back-door approach.

In addition to suing my auto insurance company, Layla also personally hit me with a 1.5-million-dollar lawsuit where she was claiming all kinds of injuries, both physical and psychological and she was also claiming loss of income due to her injuries, all which she stated came as a result of my failure to properly and safely operate an automobile.

As for Mashonda, I had gotten word from Meagan that she was seeking to sell a story to the media in which she was gonna say how me and her did cocaine, and had wild sex just hours before I crashed.

Both Mashonda and Layla were pissing me the fuck off on one hand, and on the other hand I felt really hurt by the both of them. My attorney had reached out to both Mashonda, Layla and their attorneys because he was desperate to work out a settlement deal to get both of them to go somewhere, sit down and shut the fuck up.

"Lance, if Mashonda's story gets out into the media you are screwed, and your credibility is shot and you can kiss a plea deal good-bye. The district attorney is not gonna deal. And with Layla, she was in the car with you, so we need her to corroborate our asthma story, and if not we have no strong defense and you're looking at the worst-case scenario that I laid out to you three months ago."

I sat there and contemplated what I should do. Being that I had asthma and I did have my asthma pump in my pants pocket at the time of my accident, to raise doubt in a jury's mind, my attorney was going to claim that the cold weather had triggered an asthma attack and that I was panicking because I couldn't breathe, and my asthma pump didn't help me. I had blacked out from lack of oxygen and that was what also aided in my car crash. And in addition, my attorney was gonna state that I had the cocaine on me but I didn't have it in my system. Since the cops had only tested my blood-alcohol content, which was two times the legal limit, and they didn't test my blood for controlled substances, it meant that unless the district attorney had an eyewitness who saw me using cocaine, they could never argue that I was high on coke.

However, with Layla and Mashonda suing me, we knew that we had to keep both of them happy or risk them throwing water all over the defenses that we'd planned to use, especially since they were both direct eyewitnesses, not to mention mistresses.

"So what do you say I do?" I asked my lawyer.

"You gotta come up with the cash," he said matter-offactly. "The best I can do is negotiate the best terms possible for you in a settlement agreement."

I couldn't believe how shit was just crumbling and falling down around me with each passing day. I mean, the math just wasn't adding up in my favor. Including my current attorney and the attorney that I had when Nicole had me locked up, I had shelled out close to twenty thousand dollars in attorney fees, and I hadn't even gone to trial yet! Plus, I had cash tied up to secure my bail. And over the next two weeks my attorney had reached a fifty-thousand-dollar settlement with Mashonda just so she would keep her fucking mouth shut about me and the cocaine. The deal that we reached with Mashonda was under the guise that I was buying her life rights with the exclusive and sole purposes of creating a movie script or a book manuscript at my discretion. And under the deal that was not allowed to be disclosed by either side, there was a bullet-point list of things that Mashonda was not allowed to discuss with anyone, including the media. As for Layla, I had to shell out a hundred thousand dollars in order for her to settle her lawsuit, which—like Mashonda's—also came with a strict confidentiality clause.

Those big hits of cash were having a really big effect on my pockets. I wasn't starving but it definitely didn't feel good at all. But it had taught my ass a really good lesson, a lesson that I had already known, and that was that no pussy was ever really free.

Chapter Thirteen

It was now the middle of May. Four months had passed since I had been involved in the fatal car crash. As time progressed I was getting more hopeful that a plea deal was gonna be worked out with the district attorney and the families involved in the accident. The guy who I had critically injured in the accident had finally been released from the hospital. He would have to go through extensive rehab, but he was going to make a full recovery.

As time passed I continued on the straight and narrow. In fact for the past two weeks Nicole and I had started going to marriage counseling once a week for one hour per session. The marriage counseling helped, but in some sense it was a huge waste of money simply because the marriage counselor was discussing things with us that we already knew. We had been married for more than a decade and during that time we had seen it all, done it all, and experienced it all, so although he tried his best and I was committed to continuing on with it, I just wasn't certain how helpful it would be for us in the end.

"So, Lance, in your mind, tell me what you think the biggest problem is in your relationship?" the marriage counselor had asked me during our first session.

I contemplated his question before proceeding to answer.

"Listen, I know I have issues and a lot that I could do better, but if you want me to get at the root of things I would definitely say that it's the lack of sex."

When I said that, Nicole began squirming in her chair. The marriage counselor immediately told her that she had to watch her body language so that she wouldn't encourage a hostile environment, which wouldn't facilitate openness and honesty.

Nicole apologized and I continued on.

"Like, in all due respect, we don't even need to be here. All me and Nicole need to do is have more sex. When we first got married we had sex at least once a day but more like twice a day and I got breakfast in bed and all of that. But fast-forward and I'm lucky if we have sex once or twice a week! And breakfast in bed? I can't remember the last time I had that. It's like Nicole will make breakfast for our son and you would think that she would make breakfast for me too at the same time, but that rarely happens. So with the lack of sex, and the lack of attention and affection that I get, intimacy gets tossed right out the window. So what I do is I substitute the intimacy that I used to get.

I substitute it with my work and I stay at my computer trying my hardest to bang out best-selling books and then I crave and soak up the praise I get from my fans that tell me how much they love my work."

Nicole couldn't take it anymore and so she raised her hand and asked if she could interject something.

The marriage counselor nodded his head and Nicole spoke up. "Yeah, I just wanna say that Lance always brings up the same thing. But I feel like this is less about sex and more about his low self-esteem. And at the core of it, Lance is just a very, very, very insecure person and he needs so many things just to validate who he is. To me that's more of the problem."

I kept my mouth shut because there was no sense in arguing. And I made a point that through-out the marriage counseling that I would not ar-gue with Nicole, and that I would try my hardest to be cooperative. But no matter what she or the marriage counselor said, the root problem that we had is the same problem that most marriages have, at that was the lack of sex.

It was mind-boggling to me because it was so simple to solve. All Nicole had to do was fuck me two to three times a day and things would be good. If she didn't, then we would be fooling ourselves if we ever thought that we could or would dig out of the marriage mess that we were in. That was what I believed, and I believed it with all sincerity. I truly loved Nicole but I knew what I needed and sex was a really big need of mine; and if we were going to make this work then we had to increase the frequency of sex. Just like if I consistently don't eat food two or three times a day, that's gonna be a problem for me and it will manifest itself somehow. In the same sense sex to a marriage was like food to the human body.

So anyway, marriage counseling was cool, but what was scaring me was that I was starting to get comfortable again. I had moved out of my mother's crib and got an apartment in a high-rise condo building on Queens Boulevard, in the Forest Hills section of Queens. I was only renting it because with the court case looming over my head, it didn't make sense for me to go out and buy another asset that could possibly be taken away from me. And if me and Nicole ended up in divorce then that would be just one more thing that we would have to divvy up among us.

I didn't really have the apartment hooked up the way I wanted to hook it up. In fact, after living there for one month the apartment was pretty bare bones. But even though I didn't have the apartment hooked up the way I wanted it, that didn't stop me from inviting Meagan over to my place so I could chill with her.

Meagan lived in a very upscale town in New Jersey called Saddle River, so I was sure that she was used to nothing but the best. My apartment definitely wasn't the best but I didn't care if I wasn't able to impress her, I was just feeling mad lonely and I wanted her company more than anything.

"Hey, Mr. Lance," Meagan said as I opened my door for her and she sashayed her way into my apartment with some open-toe high heel shoes that she was wearing. "I bought you something," she said as she handed me two different packages.

The first thing that she gave me was a red velvet cake that she had picked up in Brooklyn from the famous Cake Man Raven. And the other thing that Meagan bought for me was brand-new king-sized bedsheets along with towels and different things for my bathroom.

I laughed and I told her that she didn't have to do all of that.

"Lance, you told me that you're living without a shower curtain. Come on, man. I gotta look out for my people," she laughed and said.

I took Meagan on a quick tour of the apartment and she said that she really liked it.

"No, this is a nice place. You just gotta give it some personality and buy some furniture and you'll be straight," she said as she walked out onto the terrace.

It was still light outside so you couldn't really get the full effect of the view that the terrace had.

"The view is sick once it gets dark," I explained.

"Is it?" she asked.

"Yeah, it is."

Me and Meagan had been talking on the phone almost every day for the past two weeks, and she was really a cool person. We had agreed that I wouldn't do the interview with her until after all of my legal issues were resolved, but yet that didn't keep us from staying in touch.

Initially, I had the impression that she was the gold-digging type, but as I got to know her I realized that she wasn't like that at all. She definitely liked high-end stuff and she made no excuses for that, but at the same time she worked her ass off and she was smart as hell, so it was like her hard work afforded her the best things in life. But what I really liked about her was that she wasn't just after trying to juice some dude—in fact, she was the exact opposite. Her thing was she wouldn't fuck with a nigga who didn't have his own and who didn't have his shit together simply because she was fearful of some dude trying to get to her heart simply so she could take care of his ass.

We had so much in common. We both shared the same zodiac sign. We both loved sports, especially basketball. We liked the same movies, the same food; it was almost scary how compatible we were.

"What?" Meagan asked when she caught me looking at her.

I smiled and shook my head and I told her that I was just staring at her because I couldn't believe how beautiful she was.

"Lance, I see how you got yourself into so much trouble. You just naturally know how to charm women and it comes across so believable."

"Believable? As in, I'm lying? Meagan, you know you look good, so knock it off."

"I'm okay," she said, trying to be modest.

"You know you're more than just okay. I can prove it."

"Prove it how?"

"By asking you a question, but you gotta be honest and don't dance around the question."

"Okay, shoot."

"When you take a shower, or when you're getting dressed or whatever, and you see yourself in the mirror. I'm talking about when you see yourself head-to-toe butterball naked, tell me yes or no, do you turn yourself on?"

"Lance!" Meagan said as she laughed and slapped me on my arm.

"See, you said you wouldn't dance around the question."

"Okay, okay, okay. See, when I see myself naked, yes, I like my body and I think I look good. I mean, I work out and I stay in shape so—"

I cut her off. "Nah, that's not what I asked you. I asked you do you turn yourself on when you see yourself naked."

Meagan was smiling and blushing from embarrassment

"All right, you win! Yes, I do get turned on sometimes when I look at my body."

"See, case closed!"

"I am so embarrassed right now," she said as she laughed. "Like, is that normal or is there something abnormal and sick about that?"

Meagan made it clear that she didn't want me to get it twisted about the fact that she was not into women.

"I mean, I might like what I'm working with, but your girl is still strictly dickly!"

"Come here," I said, smiling. I took Meagan by the hand and I guided her close to me and without asking I started to kiss her.

I could feel her resisting me and trying to pull away, but I wouldn't let her move.

"No. Don't fight me," I whispered while my eyes were still closed and my lips were still close to hers.

"Lance, I can't be kissing you. You're still married."

"Shhhhh," I said real softly and directly into Meagan's ear. I then kissed her on her earlobe and I worked my way down to her neck and I kissed her on her neck for about thirty seconds or so before moving back to her lips.

Meagan stopped resisting me and she kissed me real passionate and deep, and I could tell that she didn't want to stop, as we kissed for about two minutes straight.

When we stopped kissing, she looked at me and smiled and then bowed her head and backed away from me.

"You are trouble, Lance. Trouble."

I didn't say anything because I knew that I didn't have to say anything. Meagan was feeling me and I knew it.

It was just starting to get dark, and the crab legs that I had steamed were ready so I asked Meagan if she was ready to eat.

"Ehhh, yeah, I think that's a good idea," she playfully said.

Before long we were both laughing at the fact that I had no kitchen table and no chairs for us to sit on.

"Do you even have a couch, a chair, a La-Z-Boy? Something?" Meagan asked.

"Nah, but wait, just chill, I got this," I said and I went to my room, took the bedsheets off of it along with the pillows and I came back to my living room and I told her that we could just put that on the floor and eat Indian-style.

"You know what?" Meagan asked rhetorically as she laughed.

"It'll be cool," I said and I began placing the sheets on the floor.

Meagan took her shoes off and reminded me that she was used to eating at high-end places like Mr. Chow or Nobu.

"This is gonna be better than all of that," I said. I went to the kitchen and got the crab legs and two plates and took that to the livingroom and then I went back and got a bottle of wine and two wineglasses.

"So this is it? Just crab legs?"

"Yeah, that's all I made."

"What happened to the corn, the broccoli, the baked potato?" Meagan said in a jokingly sarcastic way. "But you know, I ain't even mad at you. This is gonna be fun. Even though crab legs is soooo *not* the thing you eat on a first date."

Meagan was right, crab legs was a messy thing to eat, so therefore it wasn't the most romantic thing to eat.

"Oh, so this is a date, then?" I asked.

"You better leave me alone," she said as she got up and went to the kitchen. "Please tell me you at least have some butter in your refrigerator."

I at least had butter, and so Meagan melted some butter so that we could dip the crabmeat into it.

"How you gonna eat crab legs without butter?" she asked as she shook her head.

It took us about twenty minutes to eat the crab legs and Meagan helped me clear the dishes and then we started watching a movie while we drank the wine and ate the red velvet cake that she had brought.

"I'm happy I came over to see you."

"I'm happy you came over too," I said as we lay next to each other on top of the blankets. The room was dark, other than the light that the flat-screen television produced.

I started kissing Meagan again and this time she kissed me back with no hesitation. I moved my hand to her ass and felt on it to see what she would do, and she didn't take offense. She was wearing a blouse and a skirt so I decided to slide my hand up her skirt and soon I was feeling her bare ass.

"I love the way you kiss me," she said through a partial moan.

I rolled onto my back and I pulled her on top of me and continued to kiss her as I slid her skirt all the way up and squeezed both of her butt cheeks as hard as I could with my hands. I could tell that Meagan was getting more and more turned on because she kissed me more and more passionately.

Before she could change her mind, I stood up and picked her up in the process and then I slowly put her back down on the floor while managing to undo her skirt, which made it easier for me to slide it off.

"You make me sick! You do know that, right?" Meagan asked.

"I'll make up for it. I promise," I said as I slid off her purple thong and buried my head between her legs and started eating her pussy.

If there was one thing that marriage had taught me, it definitely had taught me how to eat the lining out of a pussy and drive a chick insane.

Eating Meagan out was so easy to do simply because she had the biggest clit and the fattest pussy that I had ever seen in my life.

"Your pussy is turning me on," I said as I came up for air.

"You like it?" she asked through heavy breathing.

"I love it!" I said and then I went back to work sucking on her clit.

In minutes Meagan was cumming and I was feeling so good. I had seen her sexy ass on television for years, long before I had even thought about writing books, and now here I was eating her out and making her cum and about to fuck her.

"I wantchu," she said to me after she had regained her composure from nutting.

I stood up and I took my clothes off and I was surprised that my dick wasn't already rock-ass hard.

"I don't have a condom." I said to Meagan.

Meagan looked at me and she started to unbutton her top.

"It's okay. I just wanna feel your dick inside of me."

I couldn't believe her response, but I was having my doubts. That was until I looked down at her body and all logic and reasoning went out the window. If she was willing to fuck me raw, there was no way I was gonna pass that shit up.

Meagan was on the floor sitting up while I was standing up so my dick was parallel to her face. And since I wasn't hard yet I wanted her to suck my dick until I was rock hard. So without asking I moved in and held my dick right to her face, assuming that she was just gonna automatically start sucking it.

"Eh-uhm. I'm sorry, baby, but I just don't do that," she said to me.

"You don't suck dick?" I asked, real surprised.

She shook her head and said no.

Then she stood up and started kissing on my chest and my neck while she stroked my dick until it was hard. Once it was hard, I guided her back to the floor and I was gonna fuck her missionary style. But from the ten seconds that it took for her to lay down and spread her legs, my dick went soft.

"What the fuck is going on?" I said to myself.

"You okay?" Meagan asked.

"Yeah, I'm good," I said even though on the inside I was panicking like a motherfucker because never before in my thirty-four years had my dick failed me. It had always been standing at attention and ready for war. But at that moment my dick was not cooperating at all.

So I started eating Meagan out again and her pussy was dripping wet and she was still responding good to my tongue. Just hearing her moan was enough to turn me on again and in seconds my dick was good and ready to go.

"Stand up, let's do this doggystyle," I instructed.

"I wanna feel that shit," Meagan said as she stood up.

Just that quick I could feel my shit getting soft again. So I was really in freaked-out panic mode. I grabbed the shaft of my dick and was squeezing on it to try to keep it hard while I tried to slip it into her pussy, but shit just wasn't happening.

"Baby, you sure you okay?" Meagan asked me. "You can run and get a condom if you want to, it's just that I'm allergic to latex," she said, assuming that the reason my dick wasn't getting hard was because of the lack of a condom.

I knew that if anything, a condom was really gonna make my shit go soft because I always felt less with a condom. But at the same time I knew that I had to do some serious damage control and I had to do it fast. I was racking my brain trying my hardest to figure out what to say or do.

"Meagan, you know what? I'm sorry. It's not the condom thing and it's definitely not you. It's just that my mind is in another place. Earlier today me and Nicole –"

She cut me off because once I brought up my wife's name she knew exactly where I was going.

"Lance, it's fine. Don't worry. Really, it's fine. I totally understand. We don't have to do anything. We can just chill and finish the movie," she said.

I visibly blew air from my lungs and I had never been so mad with myself, or felt so embarrassed and humbled and disappointed, all at the same time, as I did at that moment.

Meagan started to get dressed and while she did I ran both of my hands slowly down my face.

"You probably would have killed me with that thing," Meagan joked as she yanked on my dick.

I looked at her and she smiled.

I couldn't tell if she had said that to try and boost my ego or if she had really bought my line of crap about my mind being on my wife. All I knew was that I wanted to find the nearest hole in the ground and stick my head in there so that I wouldn't have to face the moment that was at hand.

"A man's dick can't do what his mind ain't into," she said as she stood on her tippy-toes and kissed me on the cheek.

I nodded my head and hugged her, and all I could think about was how fucking lame I must have looked at that moment. But it was what it was. All I knew was that I had to go to the doctor ASAP because there was no way in hell that I was gonna go through that shit again with my dick not cooperating.

Chapter Fourteen

It was now the first week in June. Two weeks had passed since my non-performance incident with Meagan, and what was wild was that since that incident she had started calling me more than ever, just as Steve had predicted she would do.

Steve laughed his ass off at me when I told him what had went down between me and Meagan. But he reassured me that I just had a case of whiskey dick.

"That shit happens to the best of us. But I guarantee you that Meagan is gonna be calling your ass much more now that that shit happened on her watch."

I looked at Steve kinda confused.

"See, you gotta understand that her head is gonna be fucked-up. You walking around mad as hell at yourself because homeboy wouldn't work when you needed him to. But Meagan is walking around, feeling mad, inadequate, right now. She's feeling like she wasn't hot enough, she doesn't turn you on, her pussy is whack, all of that shit is running through her head. So until you fuck the hell out of her, she is gonna be calling you just to reassure herself that you're not completely done with her."

I didn't think Steve was right at the time, but when Meagan started to call excessively and kept wanting us to go out and asking if she could come over again, I knew that Steve had hit the nail on the head.

I would speak to Meagan on the phone at length, but not once did she bring up my whiskey dick. But I made sure to duck her and make excuses each time she tried to hook up with me. I ducked her for two reasons. One reason was because--regardless of what Steve had been saying--I still wanted to speak to my doctor so I could know for sure what the deal was with me and my limp-dick syndrome. And the other reason that I had been ducking Meagan was because my lawyer had informed me that it was looking highly likely that we were going to be able to work out a favorable plea deal. I had been praying for a good outcome and I didn't want to jinx myself by messing with Meagan.

It was funny how with me it always took some kind of tragic shit to get me to focus on doing what was right. But I had begun to pray like I had never prayed before. I prayed about five times a day for God's mercy concerning my case, and it was looking a lot like my prayers were gonna be answered.

On June Eighteenth, almost six months to the day since I had the accident, my lawyer called me and told me to come into his office as soon as I could. When I hung up the phone with him, my heart was beating a mile a minute because I didn't know if he had good news for me or bad news. So without hesitation and without calling him back and asking him why he wanted me to come in, I had Steve come scoop me up and take me over to see him.

"Mr. Thomas," my lawyer said with a smile on his face when I walked into his office.

"All I wanna hear is good news," I responded.

"I learned from day one on this job that you always deliver good news in person and bad news over the phone. It usually works out better that way."

I nodded my head and chuckled at my lawyer but I was ready for him to cut the small talk and get right to the matter at hand.

"So it looks like we had an ace in the hole that'll keep you outta jail."

Immediately a smile came across my face and I instantly felt some relief sweeping through my body.

"Really? So what was the ace in the hole?"

"Olivia Rodriguez's family," my attorney said as he got up from the conference table.

"Apparently, Olivia's family is extremely religious and they came to the conclusion that this entire ordeal was God's will. They felt to recommend jail time for you would be undue justice and it would show vindictiveness on their part."

When I heard those words, I almost fell off of my chair.

"Are you serious?"

My attorney nodded his head.

"Well, what about the other family?"

"They have the complete opposite disposition of the other family. They want jail time for you."

"Really? But I mean—I thought he had recovered and was doing much better," I said. I didn't know how to feel. I just couldn't understand how the family who had lost their family member could recommend no jail time, and the family with the survivor of the accident could want to go so hard.

"That's definitely working in our favor, but I can tell you this—and this is part of the reason why I asked you to come in—I can tell you that the only way that they're gonna be willing to bend is based on dollars."

"What do you mean?"

"Lance, this is gonna come down to money. The family is being advised by an attorney and I'm sure this is a tactic for them to be able to up the ante."

I was confused because I wasn't sure what my attorney was getting at.

"Your car insurance policy is gonna pay out the max that they can pay out based on the limits of your policy. So after paying for Mr. Anderson's medical bills, the insurance company will have about a half a million dollars to split between the two families. And although two-hundred-fifty thousand dollars is a lot of money, how things are gonna be viewed by Mr. Anderson's family is that with no jail time, there really is no form of punishment that would cause the prevention of such accidents in the future. And therefore they'll want you to pay a staggering amount of money that will serve as a form of punishment for you."

"Basically, you mean punitive damages?"

My attorney nodded.

"So when you say *a staggering amount,* what does that mean in terms of real money?"

"Well, to put it in everyday language, it's gonna be an amount that breaks you."

"Over seven figures?"

"Definitely."

"Whoa," I said.

"Lance, you gotta look at it like this: Your accident took someone's life and hampered someone else's life in a major way. Then you have to look at the fact that you had a couple ready to get married and in a flash that's taken away, so all of those variables come with a value attached to it. And you also have to look at the fact that unless these charges are knocked down under a plea deal, you're looking at twenty-five years in prison, and there is no dollar value that you can put on your freedom."

My attorney wanted to get a snapshot picture of all of my assets so that he could see what I was working with and what my viability would be in terms of being able to compensate the victim's families.

Like most people, a lot of my net worth was tied up in my house. My house was valued at 1.2 million and there was about four hundred and fifty thousand in equity in the house. I had a little over one hundred thousand in liquid cash, and I still had two luxury cars that I owned that together were worth over a hundred thousand. And then of course I had the books that I had written and the royalties that those books brought on a yearly basis.

"I can tell you that I'll go as hard for you as I can and try to get them to take a half a million dollars, but they are gonna counter that by asking for a minimum of one million dollars."

"But I don't have that. So does this mean that I have to sell my house and all the shit that I own?"

"Well, not necessarily, but your lifestyle may change, make no mistake about that. You'll likely have to take out another mortgage on the property in order to pull out the equity, and your cars are gonna have to go."

"But that still doesn't get me to the million dollar figure."

"I understand that, and that is where we have a little leverage to keep you out of prison."

"You're losing me," I said to my lawyer.

"If we ultimately settle on one million dollars, you'll pay half of that in cash and the other half you'll pay over the course of five years. But what we'll argue is that you need to be out of prison to facilitate earning the money to pay off the settlement amount. Meaning if you're locked up, you can't properly promote your books, you'll likely never get another publishing contract, and therefore to send you to prison would punish

you, but it wouldn't be an all-encompassing punishment that also adequately served the needs of
the victims."

I paused for a moment and didn't say anything.
All I could think about was how one decision, one
bad decision on my part, was in an instant going
to reverse a ton of hard work on my part.

"Lance, twenty-five years in prison is the al-
ternative."

I looked at him and I knew that I wasn't built
for prison. As I sat there, I remember the news
stories right after the accident. I remember
seeing the pain, hurt and anger that the family
members of the victims had expressed at a few of
the news conferences. In my heart, I knew that
no amount of money would be just punishment
for me, so if that was the only hardship that I
would have to endure, then so be it. I would
endure it and I would endure it, gracefully and
humbly.

Chapter Fifteen

Nicole had admirably gone above and beyond her call of duty as a wife. While she had exhausted every ounce of energy and hope that she had in trying to preserve our marriage, at the end of the day she was a human being and all human beings are limited. For Nicole, in spite of the marriage counseling that we had been going to, she ultimately had enough and decided that she was going to go through with the divorce once we had been separated for one year, which was the legal procedure in New York.

I understood Nicole's decision, and I wasn't bitter about it. I was very disappointed, but after all that I had put Nicole through throughout the years, there was no way I could have any kind of resentment toward her. All I had was love and admiration for her.

I can't say that I blamed her, especially after I delivered the news to her that everything that she and I had built together in terms of our home and our savings were about to be wiped out due to the settlement agreement that I had come to with my victims and their families.

The last Wednesday in June was the last day of school for my son LL. And unfortunately I couldn't be there to pick him up because I was at a press conference at the district attorney's office. Not being there for LL ate at me and I knew that I had to really start making time to rebound with LL or risk him starting to see me in a less admirable light.

At the press conference, the DA was basically informing the media about the terms of the settlement as well as the plea deal that had been reached, and it was at that press conference that I, for the first time, had got a chance to publicly address and apologize to the families. It was funny that I was a full-time writer, so usually I was good with words, but in this case I had no idea what I was going to say. I had stayed up all night long trying to come up with the right words to say, but I continually drew blanks. Yeah, I didn't know what I was going to say but I knew that I would speak from the heart. I blew air from my lungs as I approached the podium to speak.

"I promise to be brief, simply because there are no words in the human language that can truly express what it is that I would like to say to the family and friends of Olivia Rodriguez and also to Ryan Anderson and his family and friends as well. But let me start by saying from the bottom of my heart, I apologize and I am deeply sorry for the pain and destruction that I know I have caused anyone and everyone involved in this ordeal. Particularly, I want to apologize to the Rodriguez family and to Ryan Anderson." I paused and had to compose myself because I was seconds from getting choked up. Then I continued on.

"On a cold and snowy night in January, after a night of partying, I admittedly behaved out of control like a child: Not like an adult, or like a husband, or like a father. I didn't even behave like a man. I was a coward on that night. And like a coward I got behind the wheel of an automobile while being under the influence alcohol, which impaired my ability to drive and which ultimately lead me to driving my car in the wrong direction on Flatbush Avenue, where I struck and killed Olivia and badly injured Ryan, as well as injured a young lady who was riding in my car, and for that I am beyond sorry. But my vow and pledge is to make amends to both families to the best of my ability and I will work as hard as I can to educate people on the ill effects of drinking and driving. This ordeal is not about me, it's about the victims and therefore I will end my statement by once again expressing my deepest sorrows."

I stepped away from the podium and I immediately walked over to Ryan Anderson and I stuck out my hand. My heart pounded and truthfully I expected him to stand up and punch me in the face because that was what I deserved. But Ryan was graceful. He stood up and he extended his hand to mine. I gripped his hand and while I gave him a ghetto hug and embraced him, I spoke into his ear while all of the photographers in the room flashed cameras nonstop.

Only Ryan could hear what I was saying. "Ryan, I'm sorry, man. I took something from you that can never be replaced. You did all the right things and you didn't deserve this. I want you to know that you'll always be more of a man that I ever will be. And this is a burden that I will carry for the rest of my life."

I stepped away from Ryan and he sort of had a twisted look on his face. He looked at me and nodded his head but didn't say anything.

I totally understood Ryan's reaction toward me because I was sure that he wanted to knock the shit out of me.

I then took my place next to my attorney and waited for the press conference to conclude. Once it was over the media swarmed me and they asked me what I had said to Ryan.

"I just apologized to him and told him that he was more of a man that I was."

"Mr. Thomas, I noticed that your wife isn't here. Is it true that you two are going through a divorce?" another reporter asked.

"I'd rather not comment on that, but I will say that my wife is also a victim in this whole ordeal."

"Is there anything else you'd like to say to the victims?"

"Well, this isn't about me, like I already said, so with all due respect I would just like to have the attention squarely where it should be and that is on the nature of what I did. Drinking and driving is wrong and I'm going to work to prevent accidents, such as the one I caused, from happening. That's really all I have for you guys, so if you don't mind I'm gonna be on my way."

I had already signed the settlement agreement earlier that morning before the start of the press conference. Where we ended up was I would pay a total of 1.3 million dollars, with 1.1 million going to Ryan Anderson and the other two hundred thousand going to a charity that Olivia's family would choose. I had thirty days to come up with a half-million dollars and then on each August First, starting in the following year, I would have to make a payment of two-hundred-thousand-dollars for the next four years. And as a form of security, I had to sign off and okay that fifty percent of all of my future advances and royalties would be paid directly to the attorney that was representing the victims. He would place the money into an escrow account in order to ensure the victims would get their money.

"Lance, hey?" Meagan said as she walked up to me and gave me a hug.

"Hey, baby, I didn't even see you. You were here the whole time?"

"Yeah, I was."

"So, I guess now is as good a time as any for us to do that interview that I had been promising you."

"No. We got time for that. I'm not stressing it. How are you? I haven't heard from you."

"I'm good, now that this is over."

"Yeah, I figured you had a lot on your mind and so I was just trying to give you your space."

"I appreciate that. So what's up witchu? You still looking sexy as ever."

"I just been working, nothing major, same old thing."

"But I do wanna hang out with you whenever you get some time."

I looked at her and chuckled a little bit.

"What's so funny?"

I told her to come closer so I could whisper something in her ear.

"Remember when you said that your pussy was passport pussy?"

Meagan started laughing and she punched me.

"You know I was under the influence when I said that!"

"I don't know about that, but anyway, what I'm getting at is next week my son's AAU team is gonna be playing for the national championship down in Orlando and I would love for you to go with me. All expenses on me!"

"What day?" Meagan asked without hesitation.

"Well, we would leave on the fifth and we'll be back on the eighth," I said. I knew I was pretty pathetic but I just couldn't help myself. I also knew that with the 1.3 million dollar settlement I was gonna be beyond broke and that I needed to be preserving as much cash as I could instead of making plans to trick it on Meagan.

She thought for a while and then she looked at the calendar on her phone.

"Yeah, I can do that, I gotta switch some things around, but that sounds like fun. You sure that would be okay, though?"

Actually, I knew that it probably wouldn't be smart for LL to see me with another woman like that, but it was all good because I knew I would figure something out by the time July came around.

"I wouldn't have asked you if I didn't think so," I responded.

"Oh, okay. I'm so excited now!"

"Meagan, you're funny."

Meagan said that she loved going away. It didn't matter where she was going, just the thought of traveling turned her on.

"It's like the days leading up to the trip is the biggest and best form of foreplay for me," she joked.

"Okay, that's what I'm talking about. So we gonna get it on and poppin' then."

I was able to say that with some renewed confidence, because against my doctor's wishes I had persuaded him to write me a prescription for Viagra, and therefore, I knew that I wasn't gonna have another repeat failed performance with Meagan.

It was really gonna be on and poppin' and I was definitely planning on handling my business the right way this time with Meagan.

Chapter Sixteen

I had a consistent pattern in my life of being blessed by God one minute and then being set up by the devil the next minute. So, since it was a pattern that I had been through before, I should have seen the setup coming.

On July Fourth, just about a week after my case had settled with the victims, my agent, whose nick-name is Tony Bony, called me and told me that he had a verbal commitment from the publishing company for my new book deal. He was able to negotiate a two-book publishing contract for six-hundred-thousand dollars.

Six hundred thousand dollars was a lot of money. It was a hundred thousand more than I had gotten for my first contract. And although my agent was gonna get fifteen percent of that, and then the victims of my accident would get fifty percent of it, I was still cool with it because to me it was still a blessing and at least I knew that I would be able to eat a little something.

Tony Bony was a cool-ass white man who was based out of Hollywood but he was always back and forth between New York and L.A. So with his urging, I had decided to hang out with him and two of his other clients so that we could celebrate my new deal.

Since my driver's license had been revoked Tony told me that he would have a car come pick me up and drop me off after we left the club. He was a cool agent and we got along very well. He always made me laugh because whenever I signed a new deal Tony would only spend a couple hundred dollars on me but in his mind you couldn't tell him that he hadn't balled out of control and spent a few thousand dollars.

We had decided to go to the China Club near Times Square and when I got there Tony was waiting near the front entrance.

"Macaroni Tony! What's the deal?" I asked as I gave him a pound.

"Tony, this is Steve, my partner in crime. Steve, this is the super agent Tony Bony, aka Macaroni Tony."

Steve and Tony both laughed as they gave each other a pound. After a few minutes of small talk, we went inside and waited near the bar for Tony's other clients to get to the club.

Tony bought the first round of drinks and he told us that he had us for the entire night.

"Whatever y'all want it's on me tonight," Tony boasted.

In my head I laughed because I knew that Tony was about to earn ninety-thousand-dollars off of my black ass so in actuality the night was really on me.

"I got that candy if you want some," Tony hollered into my ear over the music.

"Nah, I ain't fucking with that shit. It already got my ass in enough trouble."

"I got a car for you! You don't gotta worry about that old shit. You party with me, you party right and you party safe. Come on, Lance," Tony urged.

"Nah, I'm good," I said and I was proud of myself for standing up and being man enough to say I wasn't fucking with no cocaine.

Just as Tony started to tell me about these white chicks and these Asian chicks that he had coming through to meet up with him, I turned and looked and I see Steve hugging on some chick and immediately I knew that it was Felicia, who was Mashonda's cousin.

"What the fuck?" I said out loud but not loud enough for Steve to hear me.

"Yo, Lance," Steve hollered out to get my attention.

"You remember her?"

"Hey, Lance," Felicia said to me while trying to give me a hug. But I blocked her from giving me a hug and I walked off to the side and motioned for Steve to come talk to me for a second.

"What the fuck is she doing here? And I know Mashonda isn't with her."

"I told her to come through. You know I'm fucking that."

"Nah, I didn't know you was fucking her, but why would you be fucking her and why the hell would you tell her to come to the club if you know about my issues with Mashonda?"

"Man, fuck all that bullshit!"

"Bullshit? That bitch cost me fifty gees!"

"Lance, just chill, nigga."

I walked off and I was vexed like a motherfucker. That was a bitch-ass move that Steve had pulled because as far as I was concerned, I was the type of person where I just believed if I wasn't cool with somebody it meant that I also wasn't cool with that person's crew of friends as well. And so that meant by default that any of my close friends should fall in line and also not be cool with somebody just to show their loyalty to me.

"Lance!" Steve said as he caught up to me.

"Steve, listen, I'm gonna just chill with Tony and you do your thing. Just do you."

"Yo, Mashonda's moms is coming through too, you—"

"What the fuck? So this is just gonna be one big family reunion?"

"Lance, just hear me out. Mashonda got over on you, but so the fuck what? Her moms is on your dick too. So, just fuck the moms and that's how you can get back at Mashonda."

"What are you talking about?" I asked Steve.

"Felicia told me that Joy wants to fuck you. And if I was you, I'd definitely hit that."

I paused for a moment and finished my drink before responding. I was really getting tired of the drama and the bullshit. I mean, I was who I was and I did my thing but I didn't need more bullshit in my life.

"Steve, I don't trust them bitches. You can fuck with them if you want to but they ain't getting my ass twice."

Just as I said that, Mashonda's mother walks up to me and Steve and she said what's up to Steve and she gave a kiss on the cheek.

"I wanna talk to you," Joy said to me and she took me by the hand and pulled me to the side.

I had to admit that Joy was looking good as hell. She was wearing some white booty shorts, white high heels, and a white top that showed off her cleavage.

"I just wanted to tell you that shit Mashonda pulled that shit wasn't right. I tried to talk to her but "

"Joy, it's all good," I said as I cut her off. "Listen, I'm gonna be right back. My agent invited me here and I don't wanna be rude."

I walked away from Joy, Steve, and Felicia and I had no intentions of fucking with them for the rest of that night. But I had to admit that Joy did not look like a woman who was in her early forties. And if things hadn't gone down the way they had with Mashonda getting over on me, I woulda fucked her mother in a heartbeat.

About an hour later, I found myself surrounded by some of the most beautiful white girls that I had ever seen. And I don't know who in the club had been paid off, but someone must have, because right where we were partying, the white chicks and the Asian chicks were snorting lines of cocaine as if it were legal.

"Didn't I tell you I know how to party?" Tony said to me as he gave me a pound and handed me something with the same hand that he had given me a pound with.

I looked in my hand and saw a pill.

"It's X!" he shouted into my ear.

By that time the liquor had gotten to me and I knew that I should probably leave before I ended up in trouble that I didn't want to be in.

"You're about to sign a six-hundred-thousand dollar deal! You're allowed!" Tony urged.

This was definitely one of those moments from the old school cartoons where there was a devil on one shoulder and an angel on the other shoulder. The devil was telling me to fuck everything and to live it up and have a good time. But the angel was trying very hard to remind me that the last time I was in this position, someone ended up dead and that I needed to be smart.

"Nah, I'm good," I said to Tony. I was feeling good that I had listened to the angel on my right shoulder.

"You're joking, right?" Tony asked.

I didn't immediately respond and he was persistent.

So with his urging, I popped the pill into my mouth and swallowed it. That had been the first time I'd tried Ecstasy so I wasn't sure what to expect. But after about ten minutes, the music became louder to me and everything just felt much more intense in a very good way. And I was feeling better than I had ever felt in my life. It was almost as if I was having a nonstop orgasm—that was just how good I felt.

I started dancing with a white girl who I had been staring at the entire night. She had some big titties, no ass, and no rhythm, but it didn't matter at all. All I knew was that she was sexy as shit with green eyes and blond hair. And without even saying two words to her, I just leaned in and started tongue kissing her while I was dancing with her and it wasn't just a quick kiss, it was more like a three-minute deep-tongue kiss. I felt so good and so horny that I was thinking about trying to undress her and fucking her right there on the dance floor.

She pushed herself away from me and gave me a smile and told me that she would be right back.

"What's your name?"

"Angela," she said as she walked away.

"I see you having a good time now!" Tony said to me as he gave me another pound and at the same time put another E pill in my hand.

And without hesitation I popped another pill in my mouth and then a few minutes later I remember dancing and guzzling a bottle of Moët. Steve caught up to me and I was sure that he could tell that I was in a much better mood than I had been in.

"You good?" Steve asked.

"Yeah, yeah, I'm good. Just trying to bag me a little snow bunny," I said as I gave Steve a pound.

"That's what's up! But you need to leave with my ass and handle your business with Joy."

Right as Steve said that, the white girl, Angela, walked back up to me and this time she initiated the kiss.

"That's the six-hundred-thousand dollar man right there!" my agent shouted for the world to hear while Angela kissed me.

By this time the club was packed to capacity and it was real hard to move. But I did feel somebody grabbing on me.

"Lance, where's your phone?" Joy said to me.

I just looked at her like she was stupid because now she was fucking up my high and she was cock-blocking what I had going on with Angela.

"Joy, I'm good. I'm good," I shouted over the music. I was hoping that she got the hint that I wasn't trying to take her number or give her mine.

"Take my number and make sure you call me," she said.

Right at that moment, Angela bent down on the dance floor and she unzipped my pants and started sucking my dick right there on the dance floor. It was dark so it was hard for anyone to see what she was doing. The strobe lights would bring bright light to our area every so often, and when it did, I was sure that everyone in that immediate area knew what was up.

"Yo, I'll get it from Steve later on. Just make sure he has it, a'ight?" I said to Joy as I saw her standing there with her phone out as if she was about to put my number into her phone.

"Oh, oh, okay," she said with a surprised tone like she had finally gotten it. But I also think that she saw Angela sucking my dick and that was how she got the message.

I hoisted the bottle of Moët to my mouth and guzzled it some more and I knew that either the E pills were a natural aphrodisiac or that Angela had the best head game in the world, but I felt like it was only gonna be another few minutes before I came. Angela stood up and I wanted to push her head right back down to my dick because I definitely didn't want her to stop.

"This is what I had walked away to go and get," Angela said to me as she pressed up against me and handed me a condom.

A big smile came across my face and I asked her if she wanted me to put the condom on right then and there.

She didn't say anything, but she did turn around and backed her little ass up into my dick.

So I took that as my cue that she definitely was ready to get fucked right then and there. I put the bottle of Moët on the ground and I quickly slid the condom over my dick and slipped my dick under Angela's dress until I found her wet spot. She wasn't wearing any panties so that gave me easy access to her tight pussy.

Angela was slightly bent over and it looked as if we were just dirty dancing and grinding on each other. But there was a whole lot more going on. I was fucking a white girl for the first time in my life and it was easily feeling like the best pussy that I had ever had. When I finally bussed after about three minutes, I felt like I was gonna black out, simply because I had never came so hard in my life.

Right at that moment, as good as I felt, I knew that my life wasn't just out of control—it was dangerously out of control! And I also knew that just as surely as God had blessed me with a new contract for six hundred thousand dollars, that the devil had been right there lurking and waiting for a chance to bring me down. The only thing was that I just had no idea how closely the devil had truly been lurking.

Chapter Seventeen

The car that my agent had taken me to and from the club was the best thing in the world, because by the time I left the club at three in the morning I was in no shape to drive. And what was worst was that by the time I got home I was feeling sick as a dog, but I couldn't go to sleep because I knew that I had to be back up at six that morning so that me and LL could go to the airport for our trip to the basketball tournament in Orlando.

After taking Alka-Seltzer and eating a ton of oranges, I dragged myself into the shower and stayed there for about a half hour. I really felt like shit. Hangover didn't do me any justice in explaining how bad I felt. But as I walked into my room and gathered clothes to bring with me on the trip, I knew that laying down on my bed even for just a second would be the worst thing in the world for me to do. My cell phone started to vibrate and I didn't even have the energy to walk over to the phone, but I eventually answered it.

"Hey, just checking to see if you were up," Meagan said on the other end.

"Thank you. Yeah, I'm up. I'm getting ready now," I said, trying my hardest to mask any of the hangover effects.

"Lance, I am so excited. And you know, I never told you this, but I have never even been to Disney World," she said. She was sounding way too cheery and way too chipper, especially since I had the worst pounding headache in the world.

We spoke on the phone for a little while longer and before we hung up I confirmed everything with Meagan and told her that I would see her when I got to the airport. I had purchased a round trip plane ticket for her so that she would be on the same plane with me and LL and the rest of the team, but I made sure that she wasn't seated next to us. I also booked her hotel room in the same resort that we were staying at, only we were on the fifth floor and she would be staying on the sixth floor.

My plan was to keep Meagan away from LL as well as away from any of the other parents of the kids who were on his team. And being that she was only going to be one sleeping one floor above me, I was planning on going to her room when LL went to sleep and also when we took the kids to Disney World I was gonna make it where

Meagan would be there already and then I would just bump into her as if it were a coincidence. Since Nicole couldn't make it down to Orlando, I didn't want LL to see me with any other females because I was really worried about the message that I was sending to him. I mean, as fucked-up as I was I didn't want LL to grow up and be even remotely like me.

As time was flying by, Nicole called me and told me that LL was up and dressed and ready to go and that she would be at my apartment in twenty minutes to take us to the airport, being that I couldn't drive.

When Nicole arrived I got in the car, trying my hardest to be as normal as possible and not let on to my hangover.

"Hey, what's up, superstar?" I said to LL, who was dressed in full LeBron James gear.

"You supposed to call me MVP," he said, correcting me.

"LL, what did I tell you about that?" Nicole said as she turned down the radio.

"I know, Mom, but I'm just doing what we learned in Sunday school. They said that we can speak things into existence and since I wanna win the MVP at the tournament, I'm speaking it into existence."

I looked at Nicole and all I could do was smile. And at the same time I wished that I was as focused on God as my eleven-year-old son was.

"You okay?" Nicole asked.

"Yeah. I'm good. Just real tired. But I'll sleep on the plane, so it's okay."

"Well, they don't have any games or anything today, do they?" Nicole asked.

"Nah, today and tonight is a free time for them. So we'll probably hang out in the hotel until about three o'clock and then we'll take them to the amusement parks. This way it's not just about basketball and then tomorrow they have their semifinal game, and if they win, then the next day they'll play for the championship," I explained.

LL then spoke up and he said that his coach told the team that the past MVPs of that tournament all ended up in *Sports Illustrated* and that they were ranked in the top twenty-five sixth graders in the country.

"You know, Lance, see, this is a little crazy! Why are they ranking kids in the sixth grade? Why don't they just let them play the game and have fun? This is exactly how these athletes get so spoiled and walk around like the world owes them something. It's because of being told that they're all of that from the time they can walk."

"It is what it is." I replied. "But there's also gonna be college scouts there."

"For sixth graders?" Nicole said with a laugh.

Nicole really didn't understand just how good LL was. He was playing for an AAU team called Riverside. And he wasn't just on the team, he was one of the stars of the team. So with Riverside's history of producing some of the greatest players to ever come out of New York City, LL was pretty much a shoo-in to get a basketball scholarship in six years.

We finally arrived at the airport and Nicole pulled to the curb. She got out of the car and gave me a hug and a kiss on the cheek. Then she hugged LL real tight. And even with the crazy hangover that I was feeling, it didn't prevent me from feeling real nostalgic like the three of us were a family again. I loved that feeling.

"Be good," she said to LL.

"Okay. I love you, Mommy," he said as he threw his bag over his shoulder and whipped out his PSP.

"I love you," Nicole replied.

"Nicole, I'll call you later on," I said before me and LL walked into the terminal.

It was a little past six-thirty in the morning and our flight wasn't until 8:00 A.M., so after we checked in me and LL waited at the flight gate and as he played with his PSP I got a little emotional because I wished that I could just do right and not feel this need to constantly step out on Nicole. Like I knew that I was so blessed and yet I was always fucking up those blessings. Yet at the same time, I was who I was and therefore it was hard for me to change. But it was clear that God had wanted it just one way and that was with the family unit intact. I knew that had I just always stayed focused and done right, that this trip to Orlando would have been ten times more fulfilling for me than it was. It woulda been more fulfilling simply because I was proud of my son for so many reasons that extended beyond basketball, and for me to be able to travel with him and support him in something that he loved to do was so much more than I deserved and could have ever hoped for. But the reason I say it could have been more fulfilling was because I knew that had LL known the true character of his father then he wouldn't have been as proud of me as I was of him.

Before long both LL and I had dozed off right next to each other. And eventually I felt a tap on my shoulder and I opened my eyes to see Meagan standing in front of me, looking sexier than I'd ever seen her look. She had some dark shades on and she had a baseball cap on in order to help hide her identity since she was a television personality. And even with the hat and the shades she still looked sexy.

She mouthed the word *hi* without actually saying anything because she didn't want to wake up LL. So I stood up and I talked to her for a minute.

"Did you just get here?" I asked.

"Yeah, I hit a ton of traffic on the George Washington Bridge. But I'm good because I just have this one carry-on that I'm bringing."

"Yo, I am feeling so fucked-up right now. I didn't tell you but I'm getting ready to sign a new deal for six hundred thousand and my agent took me out last night and we celebrated, but I drank way too much."

"Wow, Lance, that is good. I'm so happy for you. You should go get some ginger ale or something to help settle your stomach."

"Nah, I'll just chill. I'll be all right by the time we land."

After I said that to her I told her what the plan was for the kids and that I would come up to her room and see her as soon as the kids got involved in their first activity.

"Okay. I'm still so excited! I feel like a little kid on Christmas eve," Meagan smiled and said. "Lance, is that your son?"

I nodded.

"He is such a cutie. I can't wait to see him play," she said before she walked over to another area and took a seat and started reading *Essence* magazine.

We had a very smooth flight to Orlando and after the flight had landed Meagan took a cab over to where we were staying, while LL and I and the rest of the team and the parents were picked up in a chartered van and chauffeured over to the Walt Disney World Resort, which is where we were staying. Walt Disney World Resort was also only minutes away from Wide World of Sports, which is where all of the AAU National Tournament games would be held.

By the time everyone got settled into their rooms it was a little after one-thirty in the afternoon. LL was like an Energizer bunny and he was bouncing off the walls, ready to jet from the room and go have fun with his teammates. But I wanted to make sure that I reined him in just a bit so that he wouldn't get lost or into any trouble. Overall, he was a very good kid, but with the resort being as big as it was I just wanted to make sure that he didn't roam free and do anything that might have jeopardized him or his teammates.

Although I wanted to jump in the bed and go right to sleep, I knew that I couldn't be selfish and that I had to hang with LL in order to make him happy. So we left our room and went down to the arcade and played video games and pool for about an hour or so until it was time to eat lunch at three o'clock.

At three o'clock everyone on the team and parents met up in one of the restaurants that was located on the second floor of the resort. Since all of our accommodations were all-inclusive, it meant that the kids and the parents could all eat until their heart's content. And as parents, we didn't have to tell the kids twice that all of the food was free because they had a field day. They stuffed their faces with hamburgers, French fries, pizza, soda, and ice cream. It was amazing watching them eat so much food. When they were done eating everyone retreated to their rooms to rest and to let their food digest. But again, LL was bouncing off the walls and he couldn't sit still for a moment.

My cell phone rang and it was Meagan.

"Hey, just checking up on you," she said.

I went into the bathroom to talk on the phone so that LL couldn't hear our conversation.

"Yeah, I just got back to my room with LL. The kids just finished eating so we're just chilling now."

"Lance, I love these rooms! This place is so nice. Thank you so much for flying me down."

"It's no problem. Thank you for coming."

"So are you feeling any better?"

"Yeah, actually I'm feeling much better," I said. I didn't tell her that I had thrown up in the bathroom while we were on the plane and that was mainly when and why I had started feeling better.

"Okay, so just call me when you can. I'm probably gonna just go downstairs and walk around, take everything in," she said.

"Meagan, listen, LL is dying to get out of the room and go play with his friends, so I'm gonna let him go chill with them and then I'll come up and see you in like fifteen or twenty minutes."

"You sure, baby? I'm okay. Really, I am. I don't want to cramp you in any way."

"Nah, I'm good. Like I said, LL can't sit still so he's ready to get into something. So I'll be there soon."

Meagan said, 'okay' and then she hung up the phone. And before I exited the bathroom I made sure to pop a Viagra into my mouth and I drank some water from the bathroom faucet and swallowed the pill.

"Daddy, look," LL said as he pointed to the television show.

I looked at the television and there was paparazzi-style magazine show called *DMZ*.

My mouth dropped to the ground and my heart started to pound as fast as it could as I realized how Mashonda's mother Joy had played me. The show was going into a commercial break but they were saying that after the break they were gonna air exclusive footage of me that was captured on a cell phone video camera of me living it up, getting drunk, popping champagne bottles and having oral sex on a nightclub dance floor just a week after settling with the victims and family member of a deadly DUI accident that I had caused.

I turned off the television and told LL that the media sometimes makes stuff up in order to make money and that I didn't want him to watch that.

"But Dad . . ."

LL was so smart and mad inquisitive for his age and I knew that he had mad questions for me but I cut him off before he could finish talking. And that was because I still felt a ton of remorse about everything that had happened and I had never really had the chance to sit down and talk to him face-to-face and explain things to him the way I wanted. I felt that at that moment down in Orlando wasn't the right time.

"Listen, you wanna get some of your friends and go down to the pool out back?" I quickly asked, trying my hardest to change the subject by averting his attention.

"No doubt!" he replied and then went immediately to his suitcase to look for his swimming trunks.

"Are you coming?" he asked.

"Yeah, I'm coming, but I have a horrible headache so I just wanna lay down for a minute and rest. I'll be there in like a half hour," I said to him before reminding him to take a towel with him and to take his flip-flops.

"Make sure you hurry up and come," he said to me and in a flash he was out of the room.

LL had told me that he was gonnna go get his best friend on the team to go to the pool with him, a kid named Aziz.

When LL left the room I turned the television back on and *DMZ* was airing the piece on me. They were slowing down the video and zooming in on me and highlighting shit in order to show the girl going down on me while I took a bottle of champagne to the head and chugged it.

I cringed at the sight of what I was seeing and I could only imagine how damaging it would look to me once the local New York stations got ahold of the video and started blowing it up on the airwaves, especially since *DMZ* is a national show.

The only thing that I had going in my favor was that parts of the video were dark and I wasn't all that easy to clearly make out. But at the same time there was portions of the video where it was clear what was happening and the image of the person in the video clearly looked like me.

I wanted to call my agent to see if he thought it would be necessary to do any damage control with the publisher. See, the fact was I hadn't officially signed the deal and if the *DMZ* thing were to blow me up in too much of a negative light, I worried that the publisher might balk on the deal and dead the whole thing before the ink got a chance to be applied and dried.

My first instinct though was to get my ass up to Meagan's room and handle my business with her before she had a chance to hear about or see my video. But I went against that instinct and I called my agent instead. His phone rang out to voice mail.

"Yo, Tony what up? We got major problems. Hit me back as soon as you get this. I'm stressed the fuck out and need to know what's good and what you think."

I immediately took off for the elevator and headed for her room. While I made my way to her room I just couldn't believe how fast *DMZ* had gotten that video of me out to the public. The only thing that I could think of was that right from the gate, Joy must have purposely been on a preassigned mission to set me up and get some dirt like that on me so that she could turn around and sell it.

I was pissed off like a son of a bitch because I was stupid enough to have allowed myself to have been gotten by her. But I was even madder at Steve for having invited fucking Felicia and Joy to the club.

Anyway, I knocked on Meagan's door and she came and opened it right away and without hesitation she gave me a long, deep kiss even before I had a chance to fully enter the room and close the door behind me.

"I know we don't have much time so just follow me," Meagan said and she led me to the Jacuzzi where she already had it full of water.

She took off her clothes and she stepped into the Jacuzzi and instantly I knew that the twenty milligrams of Viagra that I had taken was working because my dick was instantly rock-hard and I took off my clothes and joined her.

"He's definitely happy to see you today," I said to Meagan as we both sat down next to each other and had the bubbles from the Jacuzzi massage our backs.

Meagan took her hand and she started stroking my dick while it was still under the water and I was trying my hardest to be patient, but I wanted to fuck her so bad that I couldn't wait any longer. And since I knew that we weren't gonna be using a condom I told her straight up that I was ready to fuck.

She stood up and turned her back to me so that I could fuck her from behind. And just as Meagan braced her hands on the rim of the Jacuzzi I could hear my cell phone vibrating and I knew that it was more than just a text message simply because it continually vibrated. Then finally it stopped.

Meagan turned her head and looked at me real seductively. With her eyes she was just inviting me to hurry up and fuck her. And just as I was ready to move closer to her and stick my dick in her, my cell phone started vibrating once again, and I knew that it was somebody calling to tell me about *DMZ*.

"You should answer it," Meagan said to me as I placed my hand on one of her ass cheeks.

"Nah, I'll let it go to voice mail," I said and as soon as I said that the phone went silent.

No sooner than I could see the pink of Meagan's pussy did my cell phone start vibrating again.

"Lance, just answer it, it has to be important for someone to be calling you like that."

I stepped out of the Jacuzzi and I looked at my phone and it was a 212 New York number that I didn't recognize but I answered it anyway thinking it was my agent calling me from his hotel room or something.

"Hello?"

"Lance?" someone shouted into the phone with a white accent.

"Yeah, who is this?"

"Lance, this is Coach Cohen. We need you to get down to the pool right away. There was an accident with LL—hurry!"

"What?" I screamed into the phone. I could tell from the panicked tone in Coach Cohen's voice that something bad had happened. And instantly I started putting on my clothes and getting dressed. I didn't even take the time to dry myself off or anything.

"It was an accident in the pool. We went to your room and you weren't there, and so I had to go to my room to get my cell phone because I didn't have your number memorized. Lance, hurry, the paramedics just got here."

"Oh, shit! Okay, I'll be right there!"

"Is everything okay?" Meagan asked.

"No, something happened with LL at the pool. Some kind of accident," I said as I bolted from Meagan's room with my shirt unbuttoned and with my pants falling down. I headed right for the elevator and it was indicating that it was on the first floor and I knew that I couldn't wait for it so I bolted for the stairwell and ran as fast as I could down six flights of steps. I eventually emerged into the lobby and I asked someone what was the quickest way to the pool and when I was told I headed into that direction.

When I got to the pool I saw a crowd of people and I knew that was where LL was.

"Excuse me! Excuse me! Excuse me!" I said as I pushed my way past people until I got to LL.

He was lying on the ground with his back on the ground and his stomach, chest, and face facing straight up and staring at the sun. His eyes were closed and there was a paramedic who was feverishly performing CPR chest compressions on him.

I dropped down to LL's face and I began calling his name, asking him to wake up.

"LL, it's Daddy. Come on, man, wake up! You're gonna be all right. Just wake up," I screamed and then I felt the other paramedic trying to restrain me and asking me to please step back so that they could do their job.

"This is my son! I'm not going anywhere!"

Then a police officer came up to me and restrained me and told me that for my son's sake it was best that I let the paramedics do their job.

I was hyperventilating and I felt like I was gonna pass out. The entire scene seemed surreal and like it was part of a movie or something.

"What the fuck happened?" I screamed.

LL's teammate Aziz and his mom came up to me and she was crying. Aziz told me that him and LL, and two of the other players on his team were in the pool swimming and playing and having a good time and that LL did a flip in the water. He came back up and then did another flip in the water but he took a real long time to come back up to the top. So Aziz and his friends just thought he was joking around but after a few minutes they realized that something was wrong and they ran and told the lifeguard and he jumped in and pulled LL out.

"Oh my God! I don't believe this. So how long was he underwater?"

"Lance, I don't think it was more than two minutes," Aziz's mom said to me. But when she said that I knew that she was just trying to lessen the blow to me and that it was probably more like three or four minutes that LL had been under the water.

A helicopter had landed on the roof of the building and the paramedics immediately hoisted LL onto a stretcher and put an oxygen mask over his face.

"Are you his dad?" the police officer asked me.

"Yes," I replied.

"Come on," the cop said to me as he grabbed me by the arm and we ran behind the stretcher as it made its way inside the hotel with the paramedics pushing it and moving as fast as they could to get to the elevator.

We piled into the elevator and we were then on the roof of the building, and all of us were piling into the helicopter with LL still lying limp on the stretcher.

"We have to get him to the nearest trauma unit and with the traffic in this area due to the amusement parks this is the quickest and the best way," one of the paramedics said to me.

"Is he gonna be okay?" I desperately asked.

"I can't promise, but he did have a pulse when we arrived. It was a slight pulse but it's still a pulse."

At that instant I wanted to cry like a baby, but I was certain that LL could hear me and I didn't want him to hear my crying.

"LL, we're almost at the hospital. You're gonna be okay, just hold on," I said and then I buried my head into my hands and I began praying to God like I had never before prayed. This prayer was different than when I had been praying due to the car accident situation. This time I was feeling more desperate and hopeless and I needed God to hear me and intervene ASAP.

After about two minutes or so, we were preparing to land on the roof of the hospital and I could see a team of doctors waiting on the roof. Just as we landed, my cell phone began vibrating and I saw that it was Nicole.

"Hello."

"Lance, what happened?" Nicole asked and I could tell that she was crying. "One of the parents just called me and they were crying and telling me that LL almost drowned? Please tell me that's not true? Please? Lance, please."

I was quiet and tears welled up in my eyes but I didn't say anything as I got off of the helicopter, and I was restrained as the doctors whisked LL away and into the trauma unit.

"Nicole, they just took him into the hospital."

"Lance, what are you talking about? What happened? Just tell me!" Nicole pleaded.

"Nicole, he almost drowned in the pool."

"But he knows how to swim!" she said desperately.

"Nicole, I don't have all the answers right. But listen, they used a medivac to take him to the hospital. They just wheeled him in and they won't let me go into the trauma unit. Baby, he had a slight pulse and I am so nervous and worried. Just please call your sister and get on a plane down here as soon as you can."

"Oh my lord. Lance, I can't believe what you're telling me. Not my baby! Nooooo! Not my baby!"

"Nicole, please just get on a plane and come down. I'll call you as soon as I get any updates from the doctors."

I hung up and before I knew it, my cell phone began to ring off the hook but I didn't answer it and I was only going to answer it if it was Nicole. Meagan called me. My agent called me. My sister called me. My mother called me but yet I didn't answer. I simply sat off to the side in the waiting area of the emergency room and I placed my head in my hands and I prayed nonstop. Nothing else in life mattered to me at that point and I knew right then and there that if God got me through this ordeal that I was gonna do right for the rest of my life. All that cheating shit and wild living was gonna stop right then and there. There was no ifs, ands, or buts about it. I just wished like all hell that it hadn't taken an incident such as this for me to finally draw my line in the sand.

Before long the emergency waiting area was filled with LL's teammates, their parents, his coaches, and coaches and parents and teammates from the other teams who had also been staying at the hotel. One by one they all came up to me and placed their hands on me or put an arm around me and encouraged and consoled me.

And finally after about forty-five minutes a doctor emerged from the double doors and he asked for me. I was pointed out by the other parents and then the doctor came up to me and asked me to please take a walk with him.

I felt numb as I walked with the doctor to the back. And when we were out of earshot of all the other parents the doctor stopped and he placed both of his hands on my shoulders.

"Mr. Thomas, before we go in and see your son, I just want to tell you that we did all that we could possibly do. Your son still has a pulse, but right now he is only being kept alive by artificial support. I'm so sorry, Mr. Thomas, but he went an awfully long time without any oxygen."

"So my son is gone?"

The doctor responded but I have no idea what he said.

I had the biggest lump in my throat and it felt as if someone had just took a two-by-four and whacked me in my ribs with it. And the next thing I know is that I threw up right there in the hallway of the hospital. I was light-headed and I was feeling like I was gonna faint.

Nurses and doctors ran up to console me and assist me but I shook them off of me and told them that I simply wanted to see my son.

I was escorted to the room that LL was in and I saw him with all kinds of tubes coming out of him and he looked so helpless.

I walked right up to him and cradled his head with my forearm and my hand as I placed my head on top of his.

I wept uncontrollably and I told LL how much I loved him. And I just couldn't stop telling him how sorry I was for not having been at the pool with him.

Never in my wildest dreams did I ever expect to be in the position that I was in with me seeing my son in the state that he was in. He was basically brain-dead and was only being kept alive on life support.

Numb is an understatement as to how I felt at that moment, but unfortunately as I cradled my son and caressed his head, I knew that it was my lifestyle and my selfish ways that had all but killed him. And other than the extreme amount of guilt that I was feeling, the only pressing thought on my mind was trying to figure out a way to take my own life in the quickest and easiest way possible.

Taking my own life was the only thing that I would have been able to do to make amends for the insurmountable and devastating loss that I had incurred.

Chapter Eighteen

Nicole and her sister arrived in Orlando at ten-thirty that night and they came straight to the hospital. Nicole hugged me and she seemed as if she didn't want to let me go.

"Where is he?" Nicole asked with tears in her eyes.

"Hey, Lance?" her sister said and gave me a hug.

I took the two of them in the room and Nicole burst into heavy weeping and tears.

"Baby, wake up, baby," Nicole said to LL as she held his hand and then kissed him on the cheek and on his forehead as her sister consoled her.

I gave Nicole as much time with LL as she needed and she stayed with him for about an hour before she came back to me and buried her head into my chest and soaked it with tears.

"Lance, he didn't suffer any, did he?"

"No. I asked the doctor the same thing and they said that it doesn't look like he banged his head or anything like that so from what they could tell is that he may have panicked for a minute or so before passing out but they assured me that he wouldn't have been in any pain."

Nicole sighed and she said that she hated to even think about LL being under the water and panicking.

"Where was the lifeguard? Didn't anybody see what was going on?" Nicole spoke through her tears.

"Baby, believe me, they tried. Everyone did all they could do. The lifeguard, he was here all day at the hospital and I had to persuade him to go home. He was so distraught and upset with himself."

"So what are we gonna do? Lance, we can't leave him like that if he's not breathing on his own."

That was when tears began rolling down my eyes because I knew that we had to pull the plug on LL so that he could go and be with the Lord. There was no way that we could leave him in a vegetated state like that.

Nicole and I were ready to call the doctor but we first wanted a few more minutes together with our son. Nicole went on one side of the bed and I was on the other side and we both held one of LL's hands.

"LL, we love you so much. Mommy and Daddy love you more than you could ever know," I said.

"You're gonna be in heaven, baby. You're gonna be in heaven with Jesus. God just needed a point guard, baby. You're gonna be an MVP in heaven, don't worry."

I then told Nicole that I need a few moments alone with him. And Nicole nodded her head and she left the room so I could be with LL.

I cried uncontrollably as I hugged LL's body and then I gripped his hand and I began talking to him.

"L, you know what I never got a chance to tell you? Daddy never got a chance to tell you that I was sorry. I'm sorry for disrespecting your mother the way I did. I'm sorry for being a grown-ass man and living like I was a insecure teenager. I didn't want you to see that *DMZ* episode because I didn't want you to see your daddy in a bad light. But the truth of the matter is that you just taught me what a real man is. A real man isn't a coward. A real man accepts responsibilities and a real man honors the decisions that he's made. A real man is proud to be a family man. A real man doesn't get his self-esteem from sexing a bunch of women. LL, a real man protects his family to no end. And I am so sorry, LL," I said through snot running down my nose and into my mouth. "If I had been a real man and lived like a real man, you wouldn't be in this position right now. I am so sorry. And I can promise you that you have my *word* that from this point forward I will start finally living like a real man."

I kissed LL on the cheek and then I walked back over to the door and asked Nicole to come back in.

Nicole could tell that I was crying and she hugged me and rubbed on my back as we embraced each other. Me and my wife both wept uncontrollably. It was without a doubt the worst thing I had ever experienced in my life. But I went and found the doctor and I relayed our wishes to him of what we wanted to do with LL. The doctor had us sign all kinds of paperwork and he asked us if we wanted a priest or any other type of religious professional present, but we declined that. And we also declined speaking to a social worker and all of the other procedural things that they had in place for situations such as this.

"We're at peace. And we're sure about this decision," I explained as I held my wife's hand.

And within five minutes the plug had been pulled on LL and the little bit of life that was left inside of him slipped away and went off to be with the Lord.

Chapter Nineteen

I wasn't sure where Meagan was and to tell the truth, that was one of the last things on my mind as Nicole, myself, and her sister made it back to the Walt Disney World resort. The resort was very apologetic and accommodating and they put me and Nicole in a suite by ourselves and they put her sister in a nice room as well.

"We'll have someone bring your things from your old room," they said to me. "Is there anything else that we can do for you?" they graciously asked.

"No. This is plenty," I replied.

Everyone associated with LL's team came to me and Nicole and consoled us and offered us many words of encouragement. And LL's coach informed us that they were going to withdraw from the tournament.

"No, Coach Cohen. The kids have to play tomorrow. LL wouldn't have wanted it any other way. It doesn't matter if they win or lose, just make sure they play and that they play their hearts out," Nicole said to the coach as she held his hands.

"Nicole, we are so sorry, you cannot even begin to imagine," Coach Cohen explained.

Eventually me and Nicole made it up to our suite, and we didn't turn on the television. We simply took off our clothes and laid on the bed and turned out the lights and held each other.

"Baby, this is my fault. I shoulda been there. I should have been there!" I vented in frustration as I started to cry.

"Lance, listen to me," Nicole said as she sat up. "Listen. Can you control whether or not one strand of hair grows on your head?"

"No."

"Can you control whether the sun rises or whether the sun sets?"

"No."

"Only God can control those things and in the same way only God can control life. This was God's will, Lance."

I just sighed and shook my head and continued to cry. And me and Nicole both just laid on the bed holding each other as tight as we could and we cried our eyes out for hours. Neither one of us could sleep.

I knew that Nicole was such a big person in every way. I mean, she had every reason in the world to blame me for what had happened and to be bitter and resentful, but she did the exact opposite.

"Let's just pray," Nicole suggested.

I wasn't in the mood to pray in front of Nicole. I didn't mind praying alone but I felt like praying with her required me to do some more cleaning up of myself so I asked Nicole to pray and she did. She asked the Lord to be with us and comfort us with his grace and the reassurance of knowing that LL was with him in heaven.

"Thank you, baby," I said to her when she was done praying.

"Nicole, how do we go on with life after something like this?" I asked.

Nicole didn't have the answer to that question and I certainly didn't. But just as surely as the sun had set that evening, as me and Nicole lay in the bed consoling each other, the sun eventually began to rise again. And as much as I didn't want to live, and with as much pain as the both of us were feeling, we knew that just as the sun would continue to rise and fall each day, that life would go on. So somehow, some way, we had to find the strength to continue on the journey of life as God saw fit for us.

Chapter Twenty

In the days following LL's drowning, Nicole and I had received word from the coroner as to the cause of his death. They listed the cause as accidental drowning. And on one hand, we felt relief because there were absolutely no signs of blunt-force trauma or blunt trauma of any kind, so we knew that LL hadn't accidentally banged his head or been hit with anything. Yet we were still baffled and there remained this sense of mystery because LL was an excellent swimmer for his age. He had been swimming since he was three years old, so for him to have drowned in the calm water of a swimming pool was just something that we couldn't comprehend.

The only theory that made sense was what Steve had theorized, which was that LL had likely had some type of cramp or a massive charley horse, which caused him to panic and swallow water and ultimately drown. Steve said that if LL had eaten within the hour of having gone in the pool then the chances of him having cramped up were high and that was likely what had happened.

Only God knew what really had happened, but Steve's theory made the most sense, because LL had eaten a ton of food only a half hour or so before going into the pool. And I was sure that he had never had a charley horse before, so if he had caught a cramp while in the water I was certain that the pain from that would have freaked him out. So Steve's theory made sense, but yet it couldn't be verified.

Eight days after the tragedy, we held LL's funeral in Brooklyn at the church in which me and Nicole were members of. It was a church called Christian Cultural Center. It was a huge mega-church that seated five thousand people and literally every seat in the church was filled. Although LL's drowning had gotten some media attention, and it had been mentioned during the announcements at the church during their regular Sunday services, I could have never imagined seeing the sea of people at his funeral. But for LL's sake I was grateful that they had all come out to his home-going ceremony.

Nicole and I had discussed burying LL in his basketball uniform but ultimately we decided that it would be best if he were buried in a nice suit and that was what we went with. But we were sure to put a basketball inside of the casket with him along with his Riverside Hawks basketball jersey.

His team had went on to win the championship down in Orlando and the team had unanimously decided that LL should be given the MVP award. So next to his casket stood a huge MVP trophy that was at least five feet tall. Around his neck we also placed the national championship gold medal that all of the team members had received. And what LL would have been the most psyched about was the issue of the *Sports Illustrated Kids* where his name was listed as a first-team sixth-grade all-American, which basically meant that he had been considered as one of the top five eleven-year-old basketball players in the country.

After the eulogy was given and after a highlight reel of LL was played on the church's huge television screens, and after everyone had walked by to view his body, tons of people lined up to approach the microphone and say something about LL.

Nicole and I both never had any idea just how many people LL had touched, and seeing all the love that he was receiving was the most comforting and reassuring thing for us.

I was the last one to speak and I had con-
vinced myself that I would not break down and
cry but as soon as I approached the microphone
and opened my mouth the tears began to flow.

"LL was more than just my son," I said as I
began. "In some ways he was my mentor. And I
say that because the word of God says that if we
train a child in the ways of the Lord that when
he grows up he will not depart from those ways.
And as I stand here today, I cannot take credit
for raising LL in the ways of the Lord. But without question I can dish out praises to my wife for
the way in which she trained LL in the ways of
the Lord. She did such a good job that he would
have to remind me to pray and remind me to
trust God for things. Everyone sees the accolades
that LL got for playing basketball and I often
used to get asked if I was one of those obsessive
fathers that pushed him to play. But I was never
like that. What people don't see and what most
would have never realized is that LL fully understood the power of faith and the power of prayer
and he would faithfully pray for God to make him
taller and pray to God for discipline to practice
and I fully believe that God blessed him in the
area of sports simply because of how LL relied
on God. But as I said, LL was more my mentor
than I was his, and so I want to leave everyone

with something that I think LL would want me to say. And when I say this, please know that I am saying it more to myself than I am saying it to any of you. In the word of God it says 'when I was a child I thought as a child and I acted as a child, but when I became a man I put childish ways behind me.' For all of the children that are in here today, live your life as a child. Live it to the fullest as LL did. But when you get older as I am, remember to put childish ways behind you and live like a man."

With that, I walked away from the microphone and made my way back to my seat next to Nicole and she gave me a kiss and squeezed my hand.

"That was so nice what you said," she whispered into my ear.

I thanked her and before long we were making our way out of the church and heading to a cemetery located out on Farmingdale, Long Island.

"Lance," Toni said to me as she touched me on my arm.

"Hi Toni," I said as I turned and gave her a hug and an embrace. I was glad to see her.

Toni then said hello to Nicole and I said hello to Toni's husband Keith. Sahara had been sitting with Toni's mom.

"Can I talk to you for a second?" Toni asked as she took me off to the side.

"Lance, I just want to say again how sad I am and how sorry I am for what you are going through and for your loss. And Keith and I were talking and I just wanted to let you know that you are Sahara's daddy and you're her father so it would only be right that she keeps your last name."

I motioned for Keith to come to where Toni and I were standing and I shook Keith's hand and looked him and Toni in the eyes, and I said, "what I just said when I was talking, I meant it and it applies to me. I have really been acting and behaving like a child and Keith, you've always shown me respect from day one and from day one you've always embraced Sahara and accepted her and loved her as your own. Only a man who has put away his childish ways can raise another man's child as if she were his own. And so Sahara can and should take your last name, I would be at peace with that."

Toni looked at me when I was done talking, and she looked at Keith and I could see a tear stream down her eye.

Toni then hugged me and held me tight and massaged my back with her hand.

"I love you, Lance," she said.

"I love you guys too," I said and made sure to give Keith a pound to show him respect.

***

We eventually did make it to the cemetery and the quick service that we had at the cemetery was also packed.

I thought it was hard seeing LL being given CPR, and I thought it was hard seeing him on the life-support equipment in the hospital, and I thought it was hard seeing LL's body in his casket. But without a doubt the hardest part for me was when LL's casket was lowered into the ground and people threw flowers on top of it.

I knew then that it was officially over. I wasn't living a nightmare. My son, my own flesh and blood, was really gone. But the thing that gave me peace was that I knew LL was more than just his physical body. Yeah, his physical body had been placed in the ground and it would return to dust as the word of God says, but I took solace in knowing that LL's spirit lived on and that his spirit would never die.

Chapter Twenty-one

In many ways life for me after LL's passing was just one big blur. It was a blur because I had slipped into a serious state of depression. Just about everything had been stripped from me. The six-hundred-thousand-dollar publishing contract that I was supposed to sign had been pulled off the table two days after LL's drowning. So financially I was ruined. I literally had nothing and I was still on the hook for making restitution to the victims of my DUI accident.

But the truth of the matter was I didn't care anymore about material things and money and fame and success because I knew that I didn't have the character to support those things. And until I developed my character, giving me money and wealth and fame would be like giving a three-year-old a loaded 9 mm handgun. I knew that because one night, about six months into my state of depression, I had decided to pray to God. It was something that I hadn't done in a while.

While I prayed I could remember something in my spirit telling me to just be quiet and to just be still. And as I was quiet and I was still, I heard something ask me if I was done.

"Lance, are you done?"

I nodded my head.

"I asked you, are you done?"

"Yes," I replied.

"Are you sure?"

"Yes," I replied and then I remember tears just streaming down my eyes.

"So do I have your attention now?"

I nodded my head.

"I had to break you, Lance. That was the only way that I could get your attention. But what I break I have the power to fix and rebuild."

I knew what I was hearing was the God's spirit talking to me. And while I wanted to listen, I also was very angry and I just couldn't understand why my son had to be taken from me. And I repeatedly asked God why.

"Why, God? Why? Why?" That's what I said over and over and over again as I cried and prayed as hard as I could. Unfortunately, I never got a direct answer from God as to why LL had been taken from me.

But a few weeks later the strangest thing happened.

Steve had called me and he told me that Meagan was trying her hardest to get in touch with me.

"Steve, I am so done with that life. I'm not trying to go back there," I said. I was assuming that Meagan had given me some time to mourn and now she was still gonna try and get with me. And I also didn't want to speak to her because I was assuming that God was trying to test me in some way.

Steve relayed my wishes to Meagan but then a few days later he called me back and said that Meagan had dropped a package off to him and that he just wanted to get it to me so that she would leave him alone.

Against my wishes, Steve came by my apartment and he dropped the package off to me and he didn't stay long. We small talked for a little while and then he left. The package that he brought with him was inside of an unopened FedEx envelope.

I opened the FedEx envelope and I saw a yellow sticky note that said for me to open the envelope marked number one, read that one first and then open envelope number two and read that one second. It was signed from Meagan.

So I opened envelope number one and it was a long, handwritten letter from Meagan. It was five pages long with writing on the front and back. And as I read it I quickly realized that Meagan was pouring her heart out to me and at the same time she was releasing a lot of personal things about herself that no one else knew and that she had been bottling up for years.

In the letter she explained how when she was thirteen years old she had become the victim of incest and how her dad had raped her and how he would repeatedly have sex with her up until the time she was sixteen years old and how that had screwed up her self-esteem and her sexuality. She said that it was due to the sexual trauma that she had experienced as a teenager that had caused her to do things sexually as an adult that she later would regret. Meagan wrote:

Lance, I was out of control with my sex life and I took risks and did things that I shouldn't have done. And while I blame it on what my dad did to me, it came to a point where I was an adult and I had to be responsible for my actions. And so just before you and I had gone to Orlando, I had taken the first HIV test that I'd ever taken in my life because I wanted to start living more responsible. Yet at the same time I was scared and didn't want to know the results so I waited until I got back from Orlando in order to get my results. And to my devastation the results came back positive, Lance. And that's what's inside of envelope number two. It's the results from my HIV test. I wanted you to see the original date of the test results. And I'm telling you all of this, Lance, because I want you to know that I believe in my heart that the first time we attempted to have sex that things worked out as they did because God was protecting you. And there is not a shadow of a doubt in my mind that what happened with your son was also God's hand protecting you.

You're special, Lance. I don't know what God has planned for your life but if He would protect you the way He has, it has to be for a reason. So although you and I never got to do that interview that you had promised me (smile), I think that you need to interview God on a daily basis until you discover just what it is that He has ordained for you.

Meagan didn't close the letter with her name or anything. She just ended it as she did. I opened up her second envelope and I looked at the paper and

I was floored. I couldn't believe what I was looking at. But at the same time it was like I could feel something lifting off of me.

"Wow!" That was all I could say.

Chapter Twenty-two

The day after I got Meagan's letter I went straight to the hospital and I took an HIV test of my own. And the funny thing was I wasn't nervous. I was totally at peace because I knew that whatever the results were that I would be all right. But as God would have it, my results were negative.

Right after taking my test I took a cab over to my mom's house and I asked her if I could borrow twenty-five hundred dollars until I got my next royalty check. And without hesitation or asking why I needed the money, she gave it to me.

And what I did was I took the train to New York City's diamond district and I purchased a princess-cut diamond ring, which was similar to the ring that I had purchased for Nicole years ago.

With the ring I hopped on the Long Island Railroad and took it to the Great Neck station and ultimately I ended up at Nicole's house.

"Who is it?" she asked as she came to the door.

"Baby, it's me," I said as I stood in the January cold.

"Lance? It's freezing out there! How did you get here? You should have called me first. What if I wasn't home?"

"I knew you would be home," I said as I came in.

"We need to talk," I added.

"You okay?" she asked.

I didn't know exactly what I was gonna say to Nicole but I knew that I was gonna speak from the heart.

I told her everything that had happened with Mashonda, Layla, the white girl at the club, and with Meagan.

"Nicole, something in me is broken. It's been broke for a long time and it was the reason I did what I did. I've ruined your life and I've ruined our marriage and I've taken away your son," I said as I started crying.

"Lance, stop it," Nicole said. "I'm fine, Lance, and I'm not gonna let you keep saying that you took LL away from me because you didn't. Have you made some of the most bonehead decisions that have affected me? Absolutely you have. But you have to forgive yourself for what happened with LL and try to move on."

"I know, baby, I know," I said and I began crying again. "Nicole, I don't have anything. Literally, I don't have nothing but I borrowed twenty-five hundred dollars from my mother so I could buy you a ring. . . ."

"Lance!"

"No, please, Nicole, just hear me out. This isn't game on my part or anything like that. But Nicole, I realized that you have always loved me more than I loved you because everything you ever did for me was at the expense of yourself and everything I ever did was done at your expense. And everything God ever does, like you, he does it for us but at His expense. And I wanna change, Nicole. I wanna do right and I will do right. Like Jesus, God's son, gave his life so we could live, how ironic is it that LL, my son, gave his life so that I could live? Nicole, I would *never* dishonor my son's death and spit on his grave by being unfaithful to you again. I promise that. So if you would take me back I'm gonna get on my knees right now and ask you . . . Nicole, will you marry me again?"

She looked at me and smiled and then tears came to her eyes.

"Nicole, springtime always follows winter. The wintertime in our lives is over. And just like spring we can start over again and rebuild and make things like they were supposed to be."

Nicole grabbed me and she held me so tight.

"Yes, Lance, Yes! Of course we can get married again. I love you more than you could ever know."

Nicole and I embraced and kissed and then we made it to our bedroom and we made love to each other like we had never done before.

Epilogue

Lance and Nicole flew to Hawaii and on a private sunset wedding ceremony on the beach with just the two of them, a minister and one witness, they renewed their wedding vows.

They eventually had two more children, a boy and a girl.

Lance studied to become a paralegal and then he began working with Nicole, helping her to build her law practice and within five years Nicole and Lance had built the second largest female lead minority law firm in the state of New York.

With their money they set up a scholarship fund in LL's name to help inner-city males go to college and they also built a qualified and capable team of lawyers and support staff, which freed them up to focus on their new passion and that was working at their nonprofit company called His Desires Her Desires where they helped repair and save literally thousands of marriages.

And yes, Lance did continue to honor his word, his vows, his marriage, LL's legacy, and most importantly he honored God and remained faithful to Nicole.

Lance took to heart something that his pastor from Christian Cultural Center in Brooklyn told him that remained with him for a long time. It helped him keep things in perspective and it also helped him to stay grounded and that was the following saying: In life, whatever we fail to truly repent of we are bound to repeat, only with greater consequences.

And with that being said, Lance was finally cured of his Dogism. . . . . .

ORDER FORM
URBAN BOOKS, LLC
78 E. Industry Ct
Deer Park, NY 11729

Name: (please print):_____

Address:_____

City/State:_____

Zip:_____

QTY	TITLES	PRICE
	16 On The Block	$14.95
	A Girl From Flint	$14.95
	A Pimp's Life	$14.95
	Baltimore Chronicles	$14.95
	Baltimore Chronicles 2	$14.95
	Betrayal	$14.95
	Black Diamond	$14.95

Shipping and handling-add $3.50 for 1st book, then $1.75 for each additional book.
Please send a check payable to:
Urban Books, LLC
Please allow 4-6 weeks for delivery

ORDER FORM
URBAN BOOKS, LLC
78 E. Industry Ct
Deer Park, NY 11729

Name: (please print):_____

Address: _____

City/State: _____

Zip:_____

QTY	TITLES	PRICE
	Black Diamond 2	$14.95
	Black Friday	$14.95
	Both Sides Of The Fence	$14.95
	Both Sides Of The Fence 2	$14.95
	California Connection	$14.95
	California Connection 2	$14.95

Shipping and handling-add $3.50 for 1st book, then $1.75 for each additional book.
Please send a check payable to:
Urban Books, LLC
Please allow 4-6 weeks for delivery

ORDER FORM
URBAN BOOKS, LLC
78 E. Industry Ct
Deer Park, NY 11729

Name: (please print):_____

Address:_____

City/State:_____

Zip:_____

QTY	TITLES	PRICE
	Cheesecake And Teardrops	$14.95
	Congratulations	$14.95
	Crazy In Love	$14.95
	Cyber Case	$14.95
	Denim Diaries	$14.95
	Diary Of A Mad First Lady	$14.95
	Diary Of A Stalker	$14.95

Shipping and handling-add $3.50 for 1st book, then $1.75 for each additional book.
Please send a check payable to:
Urban Books, LLC
Please allow 4-6 weeks for delivery

ORDER FORM
URBAN BOOKS, LLC
78 E. Industry Ct
Deer Park, NY 11729

Name: (please print):_____

Address:_____

City/State:_____

Zip:_____

QTY	TITLES	PRICE
	Diary Of A Street Diva	$14.95
	Diary Of A Young Girl	$14.95
	Dirty Money	$14.95
	Dirty To The Grave	$14.95
	Gunz And Roses	$14.95
	Happily Ever Now	$14.95
	Hell Has No Fury	$14.95

Shipping and handling-add $3.50 for 1st book, then $1.75 for each additional book.

Please send a check payable to:

Urban Books, LLC

Please allow 4-6 weeks for delivery